Mladen Jakovljevic is an accomplished author, football coach, leadership expert, motivational speaker, dedicated father of two sons, loving husband, and a passionate advocate for justice and the improvement of living and working conditions in this world.

Sometimes, the path can seem like a lonely and isolated road, with no clear direction or safety in sight. When we find ourselves on that side of life, it is common to feel isolated and challenged by societal norms. Mladen remained firm in his conviction that moral values and core principles would ultimately triumph over deceit, corruption, and political wrongdoing, although it may take longer. Indeed, the sense of being in the minority does not have necessarily a negative meaning; rather, it serves to balance positive forces and negative ones, as well as balance justice and wrongdoing. In the end, the author consistently strived to build an equal and fair environment, which would provide young athletes with equitable opportunities and optimal conditions for advancing their careers and lives in the right direction. Getting to the top of a mountain is a strenuous climb, frequently taking you through dense foliage. Opting for this path may result in a few minor scratches, however, upon reaching the peak, the sight is truly breathtaking. Keep going forward and never stop fighting for what is good.

This book is dedicated to my two beautiful sons, Stefan and Andrej. No matter what happens in life, remember you are beautiful and exceptional. There might be some tough times when you will feel like things are not going right, and you will be tested to the limits, but those challenging times will not last and will only make you stronger. You will make it through the storm, if you work hard over a long period, remain disciplined, focused, and committed to your goals. Tata promises you that.

Two of you are the greatest treasure in my life, and I want you to remember that always. At some point, your life directions might naturally split; you might go to different places and have different lives; you will meet your life partners and temporarily separate your paths. But always remember to keep your brother's love in your heart, even when facing difficult times. No matter what happens, be there for each other. Regardless of circumstances in life, keep going and keep fighting for what is right and good.

Together, you can overcome any obstacle that comes your way. No matter what people make you feel, no matter what other people say, remember that you are special, unique, beautiful, smart, and talented. Indeed, you will make it, I know that. God will always be there to protect you and to open new doors for you. Tata loves you.

Mladen Jakovljevic

FOOTBALL AQUARIUM

AUSTIN MACAULEY PUBLISHERS®

LONDON · CAMBRIDGE · NEW YORK · SHARJAH

A CIP catalogue record for this title is available from the British Library.

ISBN 9781035839322 (Paperback)
ISBN 9781035839339 (ePub e-book)

www.austinmacauley.com

First Published 2025
Austin Macauley Publishers Ltd®
1 Canada Square
Canary Wharf
London
E14 5AA

Table of Contents

Prologue

Football Mafia and Shark in the Aquarium

Success is always on the other side of pain; we must all step out of our comfort zones to advance in any field we choose. No pain, no gain. Even if you remain seated in a chair all day, you will still experience certain discomfort. If you remain in bed all day, you may experience pain, possibly a migraine.

Protecting ourselves from pain is akin to avoiding essential growth.

Pain surrounds us; at times, it serves as our greatest ally, compelling us to become stronger. Without experiencing pain, we cannot learn, improve, grow, or achieve success in our lives.

Any painful situation we encounter in life follows a similar process of overcoming. No matter what is in front of us, we should hold on to that challenging aspect, persist for a time, and strengthen our willingness daily by learning how to overcome it. With this mindset, we will develop greater resilience and acquire valuable, defining experiences and lessons from this pain. With a proper warrior mindset, we can confront adversity with a broad smile on our face.

Importance of Compassion, Support, and Empathy

A notable trend among many football players is to cease participation or transition to a different sport by the age of 12 due to having already achieved numerous gold medals and feeling as though they have reached their peak accomplishments. Their careers had not commenced; however, the pressure to succeed carries a hidden initial impact.

The journey of a young player is far more extensive than the achievement of gold medals itself. Instilling the right etiquette, demonstrating affection and encouragement, fostering comprehension, imparting lessons on resilience, and gradually exposing youngsters to competition are vital components of the football experience.

Unfortunately, many parents seek to fulfil their personal aspirations by imposing them on their children inappropriately. Simply winning hundreds of tournaments and gold medals is insufficient. In my role as an academy coach, my aim was to establish a safe and supportive training atmosphere in which my players could freely communicate their emotions to me. We frequently engaged in constructive discussions about enhancing various aspects. The majority of my players felt at ease confiding in me, entrusting me with information that their parents were not privy to. The strong bond between coach and player translated into remarkable success on the football field. Furthermore, our focus was not on chasing game results, yet they ultimately came to fruition. With this strategy, we achieved victory in numerous games, frequently triumphing over opponents who were perceived to be realistically stronger than us.

Climbing to the Top

Ascending to the summit of the mountain frequently involves navigating steep terrain and dense foliage. As a coach, I consistently emphasize to my players the importance of trusting the process. Success in sports demands a significant investment of time, dedication, effort, and willingness to make sacrifices. During the critical sensitive period of emotional vulnerability in children, it is essential to prioritize understanding, guidance, and support over pressuring them to meet specific achievement targets. Instead of solely emphasizing outcomes, our focus should be on fostering strength, resilience, emotional stability, and overall development in children. It involves providing support, empathizing with their challenges, and assisting them along the highs and lows of their path.

Shark Tank

A shark kept in an aquarium will not grow as large as one in the ocean. While a shark in an aquarium may only grow by 8 inches, those in the ocean can reach lengths of 8 feet or more. The growth of a shark is limited by its environment, much like your own potential. We are frequently surrounded by individuals with limited perspectives, which hinders our personal and professional development. Modifying your surroundings can lead to accelerated personal development. Similarly, possessing talent can be likened to having a shark in a vast aquarium. Placing a shark in a small aquarium prevents it from outgrowing its living space, however, transferring the same shark to the ocean allows for exponential growth.

Introduction

This fiction book is based on a true story with the three main characters, brothers Nikola and Marko, talented young football players, and the drug dealer and leader of the mafia cartel, Boris. The mafia leader enjoys protection from the government, police directors, and leading political parties. At the same time, he is using young talented football players to create profit from the transfer fees and game-fixing activities.

The book draws inspiration from various events within the football industry, highlighting the significant connection between politicians and mafia leaders, and the young, talented football players. That unbreakable bond formed the Bermuda Triangle. In the areas between those triangular regions, there are no recorded ship disappearances, as per legend. Rather, the substantial sum of money vanishes. More critically, several skilled young football players, such as the prominent character Marko, forfeit their careers and fail to realize their full potential in that Bermuda triangle.

This book illustrates the journey to unlocking our full potential and emphasizes that hard work, discipline, commitment, and a strong work ethic are ultimately more important than natural talent.

This book portrays the living environment where numerous aspiring young athletes fail to reach their full potential due to limitations within their surroundings. This motivational story delves into the deeper values that ultimately bring positivity into our lives. We must remain steadfast in upholding our core fundamental values, regardless of the environment in which we find ourselves. Our drive for success and determination to fulfil our aspirations should always surpass the challenges we face each day. Nikola, one of the brothers, exemplifies how maintaining a positive mindset and striving for greatness in challenging circumstances can lead to long-term positive outcomes.

Conversely, his brother Marko exemplifies the principle that achievement and recognition are not easily obtained without hard work and dedication.

Elevators do not lead us to the pinnacle of success in life; instead, we must often climb the stairs to reach the highest floor.

Marko ultimately placed his trust in the wrong individuals and came to understand too late that natural talent alone, without hard work and dedication, is insufficient. He chose to embrace life in the 'aquarium', while his brother Nikola successfully shattered the confines of the aquarium and pushed his limits to new, international heights.

Football Mafia

This book is a fictional narrative inspired by real events, the main characters of the book are two brothers who grew up in a difficult and complex environment, each seeking the opportunity to shine and demonstrate their worth. The two brothers held differing life perspectives; nevertheless, they shared a common objective: to achieve success, wealth, and fame.

How did they both defined word 'successful'? What does success truly signify in life? Is it measured by wealth, luxury cars, and expensive clothing? Or is it characterized by deeply ingrained moral values, a resilient 'never give up' mentality, the promotion of inspirational living principles, and a strong mindset?

The purpose of this book is to showcase the clear, unfiltered reality of certain young professional football players who came close to realizing their childhood dreams. The sweet and bitter aspects of the journey resulted in lasting harm to numerous young professional players, who failed to realize their full capabilities and potential due to a deficiency in discipline, fighting spirit, and the determination to surmount inevitable challenges along the way.

Chapter 1
Dusty Grassroots

Nikola and Marko were siblings, Nikola, aged 16, and Marko, aged 18, were identified as promising football players and recruited to join the biggest club in Belgrade.

Nikola's role on the team was as a defensive midfielder; he always demonstrated politeness and a strong work ethic, along with a commitment to achieving his objectives and goals. Nikola's impact was often unnoticed by the average spectators during football games, he did not play fancy passes or neither scored fancy goals.

However, his stamina, fighting spirit, and commitment to the team's performance were highly regarded by his coaches and other people in the football industry. Nikola demonstrated exceptional skill in regaining possession for his team through efficient tackling and precise ball interceptions.

Additionally, his passing accuracy was consistently good. Nikola knew how to intercept the ball from the opponent and swiftly advanced his team's offensive. His headers were impressive, and his passing accuracy was excellent considering his age. Most importantly, Nikola gained recognition for his exceptional running ability, covering significant distances throughout the game. Some of his coaches noted that he may not have been naturally talented in technical skills, but they acknowledged that he made up for it with his exceptional work ethic.

He consistently dedicated extra time to training in order to enhance his skills, focusing on strength, flexibility, and coordination exercises during his personal practice sessions. Nikola demonstrated a high level of focus, discipline, and dedication towards achieving his goal of becoming a professional football player. He was determined to see football as his opportunity to escape poverty and was willing to make sacrifices, therefore, he demonstrated exceptional work ethic on the field and exemplified true warrior spirit. He adhered to a disciplined routine, prioritizing sleep, maintaining a healthy diet, and dedicating extensive hours to physical fitness at the gym. Nikola was gradually honing his skills and becoming a formidable force on the football field. He would dedicate additional time after team practices to focus on individual skill development and improvement.

Nikola's natural talent may not have received much praise, but his diligent work ethic and discipline greatly contributed to his daily progress.

On the other hand, Marko demonstrated greater natural talent than Nikola. He possessed an innate ability to impact the game as an attacking midfielder. Marko had the ability to effortlessly score goals from any position on the field. He was a dynamic player known for his speed, agility, and exceptional technical skills on the ball. His work ethic on the field was lacking, but his exceptional natural abilities, impressive talent, and refined footwork made him the standout player on the team. Marko was discovered by the coach of the U18 football team and had the opportunity to participate in several friendly matches with the national team. He had a promising future ahead, with numerous friends and family members foreseeing a successful soccer career.

The primary issue appeared to stem from his poor attitude: he did not prioritize hard work, took his talents for granted, and lacked the drive to improve like his younger brother, Nikola. Marko was the leading scorer across all the youth teams in which he participated. He possessed a natural talent for reading the game and positioning himself effectively on the football field. He was also known for his charisma and outspoken personality.

On the top off that, Marko frequently engaged in arguments with his coach, hindering his progress.

Marko's main challenge was his reluctance to prioritize his personal life over his football commitments. He was a frequent visitor to all nightclubs, often staying until the early hours of the morning. Due to insufficient rest, his body lacked the necessary recovery, resulting in a hindrance to his progress on the football field. Marko desired to spend time socializing with his new friends, attend late-night gatherings, and occasionally enjoyed a few drinks on weekends. As a result, his progress in football and in-game performances began to decline and become stagnant.

Chapter 2
Corrupt Political Structure

Boris served as the president of the club in which Marko and Nikola were playing. He was a prominent figure in the ruling political party of Serbia and behind the scene, also operated as a local drug dealer. Boris possessed a notable criminal history but evaded imprisonment thanks to a lenient system, and his personal contribution to the rolling political party.

During that period, the Serbian government was employing individuals such as Boris to carry out dirty criminal assignments on their behalf. Boris served as an instrumental tool within the corrupt political establishment, carrying out the unsavoury tasks of the government.

For instance, in the week leading up to the election, individuals such as Boris received large financial funds to procure votes in favour of the incumbent political party. The government will assign and provide necessary resources to individuals tasked with mobilizing sufficient voters to secure their position in the nation's leadership. Boris was directed to work discreetly. He contacted political opposition figures, at times orchestrating their torture or abduction, in order to secure dominance for his governing political party. He was the dog displayed unwavering loyalty to the government.

Several opposition politicians withdrew their candidacy out of fear for their safety. Boris was allocated a substantial budget to secure the support of the electorate through financial means. With a prevailing culture of superficial values among Serbian youth, Boris held a revered position on the streets, admired by young individuals who he influenced to support the current mafia government through his status. Boris utilized two straightforward techniques.

Government funds were distributed in exchange for votes. Boris leveraged his street credibility to mobilize sufficient voters for his political superiors, achieving success in the process. Typically, Boris would distribute around 20 euros to individuals on the street in exchange for their votes, aiming to maintain the dominance of his superiors in the nation. The police turned a blind eye to numerous unnoticed crimes as a reward for his faithful service to the government. Boris led a highly structured criminal syndicate in Serbia, known for their advanced tactics in the importation, distribution, and sale of narcotics throughout the region.

Often, the individuals of his mafia organization went unchecked, with law enforcement even going so far as to assist by apprehending Boris's rival criminal groups, just to clear the way for Boris and ensure smoother business operation for him.

That agreement was mutually beneficial, providing a positive outcome for both the government and Boris.

One day, Boris made the decision to funnel his illicit drug money through the football club where Marko and Nikola were both players. It was all part of money laundering structural business plan. Boris demonstrated exceptional business acumen, despite his reputation as a ruthless and malevolent figure in the drug trade. He was aware that relying on drug money was not a sustainable solution, and he believed it was only a matter of time before he faced arrest, regardless of any government protection.

Boris was also set to take on the role of football agent of many young football players, with the potential for significant financial gains from transfer fees.

Selected high-ranking government officials endorsed Boris for the position of newly appointed president of a leading football club in Serbia. He intended to recruit promising young players and secure contracts as their representative or manager, potentially earning millions of euros with minimal risk.

The club's success was evident as it held the top spot in the Pro League standings. Boris discovered a method to compel multiple skilled players to sign an agreement for his 'protection'.

He was the cornerstone of talent for these skilled players.

Boris established a formidable network around himself by delegating tasks to his associates, elevating them to positions of leadership within the organization. He was increasingly assertive in his role, treating the club's bank account as his own personal funds. The Football Federation often provided a substantial quarterly payment to every professional club participating in the competition. However, Boris consistently exploited a loophole to drain millions of euros from the bank account, neglecting essential expenses such as club maintenance, electricity, coaching staff salaries, and transportation for away games.

Boris's greed was escalating as he depleted the club's finances annually. Despite being cognizant of these events, all the dirt remained under the carpet.

Chapter 3
Lunch with the Mafia Leader

It was a bright Saturday morning. The team conducted their final training session prior to the league game. Marko was on the verge of leaving the dressing room when club president Boris beckoned him over.

"Marko, would you like to join me for lunch? You're welcome to bring your brother Nikola; we can enjoy some good food together and talk about your future."

"Yes, sir, I would be happy to." "I will call my brother; please give me a moment," Marko replied promptly.

Marko quickly returned to the dressing room, where his brother Nikola was still in the shower, preparing to rinse off the soap.

"Hurry up, Nik! The president wants to talk to us about something, so you need to rinse off quickly; let's go! This is our day; he will assist us in signing professional contracts!"

Nikola observed his brother's urgency, taking his time to thoroughly rinse off the soap and shampoo without feeling rushed. Marko attempted to hasten him, but Nikola preferred to take his time.

He began dressing at a leisurely pace, disregarding his brother's urgency. After what felt like an eternity for Marko, they exited the dressing room ten minutes later.

Boris was smoking a cigar nearby, upon noticing Nikola and Marko, he smiled and quickly approached them with the invitation: "Nikola, you performed well in today's training session." You are making progress each day. "Allow me to treat you both to lunch so I can discuss some important matters, if that's agreeable."

Nikola directed a blank, cold stare at Boris while he noted his brother Marko's enthusiasm about going to lunch with him.

Shortly thereafter, the three took a brief walk to the nearby restaurant.

The restaurant 'Giovani' was situated just five minutes from the stadium. The table in the corner was exclusively reserved for Boris and his companions.

Saturday lunch was the peak period for that restaurant. Boris, Nikola, and Marko arrived, and the restaurant owner promptly attended to them.

They took their seats at Boris's VIP table. Four of Boris's bodyguards vigilantly observed their boss. The bodyguards were large and donned dark jackets, with their hands positioned inside the pockets, seemingly prepared for act at any moment, if needed. They scanned the restaurant for any potential threats. Shortly after Boris took a seat and ordered food for Marko and Nikola, two bodyguards exited and positioned themselves at the restaurant entrance, while two others remained at a nearby table. Boris had numerous enemies and required personal bodyguards around the clock.

"They are sizable individuals, sir," Marko remarked, indicating the two bodyguards to Boris.

"Indeed, I must exercise caution; some people are not fond of me."

"This is merely a precaution; no one would attempt to harm me, would they, Marko?"

Boris exhaled cigar smoke toward Nikola and remarked,

"Why the silence, Nik? Just take it easy; I'll order some wine for the both of you. A glass of fine wine with lunch won't harm you, gentlemen."

"Why have you brought us here?" Nikola suddenly inquired of Boris. "With all due respect, I am unclear about the nature of this matter," Nikola remarked.

Upon Nikola brave statement, Boris began to laugh loudly and in an uncontrollable manner.

He gazed into Nikola's eyes and started monolog: "I like you. You have the courage to address me directly in that manner. Pay attention now, young boy. I wish the best for both of you. My role is to ensure the well-being of young, talented players. I can assist in advancing your career; however, I will require you to sign documents granting me the authority to represent both of you in the market. I will serve as your manager, working to identify the best offer available. Once we secure the optimal deal for both of you to advance your careers, a small percentage will be allocated to me."

"I would appreciate your assistance in facilitating my transfer commission." Additionally, you are both aware that I have numerous connections in the football industry, which can assist in realizing your aspirations.

Boris retrieved some documents from his bag and handed them to Nikola and Marko.

"Please sign your names here, both of you." This indicates that you authorized me to identify the most suitable transfer options on your behalf. "I will become your agent."

Upon hearing that, Marko appeared pleased and cheerful, and without any delay, he signed the document promptly and handed it back to Boris.

Yet, Nikola stared at the documents in silence.

"Sign it, Nik," Marko urged him.

"Mr Boris will assist us in becoming professional players and earning significant money."

Unexpectedly, Nikola just tossed the pen onto the table without affixing his signature.

"I do not wish to sign anything, sir. I do not require that; I prefer not to have a personal manager. I believe I can manage myself independently now," Nikola stated.

"I must admit, Nikola, I am somewhat surprised," Boris replied. I am committed to assisting you in advancing your career, yet I find you unappreciative. I am not upset; I recognize that you are young and require additional time to evaluate your choices.

"I will visit you in a few days; please keep that in your mind," Boris said while indicating to his bodyguards that he was prepared to leave.

A few moments later, Boris exited the restaurant. His new BMW X5 was parked nearby.

Marko and Nikola were still seated at the restaurant table. Marko was angry; he appeared visibly distressed.

"Nikola, that was our opportunity, you idiot! How could you refuse the most influential man who makes decisions for everyone in this city? We have no future without Boris!"

"Listen, Marko, I don't want the gang leader to be my manager and representative; it doesn't sit well with my values. They are seeking specifically the fee associated with our potential transfers. That is obvious; he has no concern for us."

Nikola clearly expressed his viewpoint and added, "If you wish to finalize the agreement with them, that is your choice, but I do not want it,"

Chapter 4
The Consequences

A few days after that lunch meeting, Boris called Marko to his office following the training session.

"You made a wise choice, young man. Please do not be concerned about your brother. He is vulnerable; his career will suffer, because no one should reject my services."

"I will support you, and you will develop into a standout player; it is essential that you heed my advice."

Marko did not attempt to conceal his excitement and happiness at Boris's words. His face turned red as he looked down at his feet. His large, brown eyes conveyed everything, reflecting his gaze toward the gang leader, Boris.

At the same time, Nikola was dismissed from the club following that lunch meeting.

Yet, he never truly considered the possibility of feeling disappointed or quitting football. Instead, his ambition to succeed intensified further. Nikola was born a fighter. His motivation was at an all-time high; Nikola awoke each day with a renewed and remarkable energy. He aimed to continually push his limits to advance to the next level and uplift his family from poverty. All the clubs were aware of Nikola's situation and the circumstances surrounding his departure from his previous club, which made them hesitant to sign him due to concerns about Boris.

Despite this, Nikola was adamant about not giving up. He adhered to a strict workout regimen and a tailored diet.

Chapter 5
Commitment and Resilience

Meanwhile, Nikola continued to train diligently. He understood the steps he needed to take in the future to fulfil his dreams and fully realize his potential.

Nikola established an excellent daily routine to maintain his fitness and stay engaged in the sport, even after Boris suspended his football career and he no longer belonged to a club.

Nikola recognized that no one could impose limitations on him. He refused to let temporary life circumstances constrain his potential. During the cold and rainy autumn days, Nikola continued his training independently. He would wake up at approximately 5 am and immediately leave his warm bed to run 10 km along the river bay. He was running to the point of exhaustion, ascending and descending the nearby rusty stairs; he was sprinting uphill until he began to vomit. At approximately 7 am, Nikola would return home to perform push-ups, abdominal exercises, sit-ups, jumps, and various stretching routines. The breakfast hour was scheduled for around 9 am.

Having just graduated from high school, he opted for a year off and decided not to enrol in any university, choosing instead to fully commit to his football career. He recognized that he needed to invest additional effort compared to others to make up for his limited natural talent and ball-handling skills. He possessed speed, agility, strength, and stamina, which are essential attributes in modern football. Furthermore, his work ethic was exceptional; he consistently pushed his limits each day, even in the absence of the club. At approximately 11 am, Nikola would walk to the nearby park with his football and juggle the ball for nearly two hours.

Subsequently, he would return home, consume meat, fruits, and vegetables, and allow himself to rest.

At approximately 4 PM, Nikola departed on his bike to the turf football field located on the other side of the city. Weather conditions did not affect Nikola; this was never in question.

The bike ride typically lasted approximately 25 minutes to reach the football field. Nikola lacked the financial resources to hire a personal coach for support, so he chose to challenge himself on his own.

Upon reaching the football field, Nikola organized a 2-hour training session for himself. Initially, he engaged in a warm-up jog followed by static and dynamic stretching exercises, as well as rapid and balanced footwork drills to enhance his coordination and agility. He would then utilize the old training cones to arrange small drills for himself. He practiced running with the ball through confined spaces, swiftly manoeuvring between the cones, maintaining ball control while sprinting, utilizing both feet, and rolling the ball in various directions. He sustained a high intensity with minimal interruptions.

Nikola would occasionally shout, cry, and speak to himself audibly. He engaged in an intense, high-effort regimen to maintain his fitness, he recognized that it would be too late to prepare if the opportunity to play football presented itself soon. He had to be prepared at all times.

In the second segment of the training, Nikola practiced goal shooting. He would complete a minimum of 100 free kicks and other finishing drills. By the conclusion of his two hours of afternoon training, Nikola was fatigued.

Chapter 6
Choice Is Always in Our Hands

Nikola had the choice to indulge in self-pity, disappointment, and despair regarding his circumstances. The alternative was to maintain a positive mindset regardless of the circumstances, continually push boundaries, and exert greater effort than ever before. He had opted for the second option, adopting the warrior mindset. Nikola was aware that his opportunity would eventually arise, and he recognized the importance of exercising patience. As is often the case in life, when we fulfil our responsibilities and maintain a strong focus and determination toward our goals, the universe will orchestrate an inexplicable alignment, elevating us to unprecedented heights.

The first rule is to never give up, as the future holds unknown possibilities. It is common to experience feelings of sadness, misery, and a lack of motivation. However, Nikola discovered a latent strength within himself; he harnessed that small part of his being to break down all barriers, refusing to accept defeat.

Nikola persevered through challenging days under that demanding training regimen. There were days when he experienced physical exhaustion, was in tears, and was on the brink of mental breakdown. He was alone in his room, experiencing distress, shouting, and striking himself. Indeed, Nikola and Marko never experienced honey and milk, particularly after the death of their parents. Nikola and Marko were compelled to mature and develop self-reliance rapidly. They relied solely on one another and faced challenges in meeting their essential financial requirements at the end of each month.

When you feel that you have exhausted all your opportunities and chances, remember always one thing—you did not.

Chapter 7
Struggle to Survive

Nikola had a neighbour, Stevan, who consistently looked after him and his brother, Marko. He was an affluent older gentleman from a wealthy family, and since he lived alone, he would visit Nikola and Marko's apartment to see if they required assistance.

One day, Stevan visited Nikola's apartment and knocked on the door.

"How are you, Nikola? Is everything alright with you and your brother? I promised your parents that I would look after both of you."

He then handed Nikola some money, saying, "It's not much, but I need to help you."

"Thank you kindly, sir." Nikola replied.

The older man appeared concerned: "And Marko, your brother..." I had not seen him for some time. "Is everything okay with him?"

Nikola's gaze fell to the floor, revealing his concern. "Marko has begun associating with some undesirable individuals; I am worried about him, as he no longer listens to my advice."

Stevan removed his glasses and stepped closer to Nikola.

"Who are these individuals, Nikola? Can you provide me with Marko's phone number? I would like to discuss this with him."

"No, sir, that will not be effective. He is now involved in the network of football organized crime. He also signed a contract with them, and they became his football managers. I am concerned for his safety and football career; he possesses considerable talent, as you are aware."

Stevan felt disheartened upon receiving this news.

"Football is less important; you must be cautious about your associations. I will locate Marko and discuss this matter with him. He is a promising young man who requires some guidance in his life."

Nikola utilized the funds from Stevan to purchase food and cover the bills. It was really tough times to endure. He frequently felt tense but maintained his commitment and determination to succeed.

Meanwhile, Marko was appreciating his new friendship with club president Boris, resided in a rented apartment situated near the football club.

Chapter 8
Swallowing the Bait

Boris requested Marko to come to his office the day after the game, for an important meeting.

"Listen, young man, I am striving to create a comfortable life for you. Shortly, I will seek for you a club in the Premier League or Italy; they will all compete for your signature."

Until that time arrives, I would appreciate your assistance so that I may also be able helping you.

Several upcoming games require for us to achieve specific scores and agreement with my business partners.

Your role will be essential in securing our previously established deals for that game. "We operate in an industry where financial considerations govern all aspects."

Marko responded with the blank expression on his face: "Is that a form of game-fixing, sir?"

"Do not be concerned, young man."

"This represents a minor contribution to the club's revenue. I will provide you with additional information prior to the next game. I maintain positive relationships with several influential individuals in this city, and at times, I am required to provide them with some guarantees prior to the game's commencement."

While conversing with Marko, Boris was rolling a 500-euro bill to ingest a significant quantity of cocaine placed on the table in front of him.

Two bodyguards were positioned behind him. While finishing the drugs at the table for a few seconds, he continued speaking to Marko.

"Would you like some? This is high-quality crystal." Our class product is sourced directly from Columbia.

"I acknowledge that you are a football player, but the small amount of cocaine will not harm you, boy."

At one point, Boris gestured toward Marko with his bodyguard. The large individual with a scar on his face approaches Marko and tosses the BMW keys to him. Marko expressed surprise and smiled in disbelief.

"Is that for me, Sir?"

"Yes, this is your new car. The new BMW is parked across the street; you will appreciate it. This is my modest contribution to illustrate your significance to our project within the club. Furthermore, I invite you to join me at the club tonight to celebrate your future career."

Marko excited and was astonished to see the car in the parking lot. He was surprised and found it hard to believe. He had a brand new, shiny BMW X6 that he could enjoy driving around the city.

He had recently obtained his driving license and was pleased to have a joy drive around his neighbourhood.

The issue arose when Marko began to indulge in daily partying, frequenting clubs where he perceived himself as a superstar. There were instances when he experimented with cocaine for the very first time. Boris provided it to him. Simultaneously, Marko was unaware that his football career was declining. For the first time, Marko participated in a prefixed football matches, and he, along with a few other players, was among the only individuals aware of the forthcoming events and their execution.

The notorious club president had ties to individuals associated with the mafia involved in the betting syndicate; they rigged certain games and invested substantial sums of money into specific game outcomes. Before he knew it, Marko developed a drug addiction, without even realizing it. His exceptional talent continued to impact the field, he ceased his regular healthy routines and individual training for several months. Marko enjoyed the new car that Boris gifted him and hosted parties in his apartment every night. His sole responsibility was to be the player tasked with ensuring a specific score in the predetermined game triangles. Boris's football club consistently occupied a mid-table position, neither contending for the top spot in the league nor facing the threat of relegation. The game fixing was going really good for club president Boris.

Chapter 9
Game Fixing Routine

Boris was selling the games to clubs competing for the championship or those striving to avoid relegation. He was raking in a considerable amount of money with that.

Occasionally, through his network across the country, he would also wager substantial sums online, betting for his club to lose.

In this crazy but efficient manner, he was receiving payments from opposing clubs while betting against his own club, typically via an international betting accounts, that were hard to monitor from the third parties.

The manipulated games appeared regular on the football pitch. Yet, proving anything in the court case would require substantial effort.

Typically, the initial 75 minutes were played without either team showing a desire to score goals. Game play was usually intense when the ball was in the middle of the field or running down wider areas. However, when the ball approached final third of the pitch, there was a lack of intent to score during the first 75 minutes.

In the last 15 minutes, the penalty would be imposed with prior agreement from the referees. Few players were involved in this scenario.

Celebrations and the display of feigned frustrations from the team conceding the goal will appear ordinary to prevent any suspicion of investigations from the crowd.

Even the match delegate, the primary official responsible for drafting the final statement regarding the game's regularity, was also receiving a portion of the benefits. Boris's extensive political engagement provided an additional layer of protection for him and his associates. Any individual attempting to investigate or expose irregularities would face the risk of kidnapping, torture, or even death.

Chapter 10
Mafia Connection
with Government

Boris maintained a strong affiliation with the ruling government party and had his associates positioned within the upper echelons of the police department and the judiciary. Boris meticulously attended to every detail to ensure seamless business operations. Indeed, he had no interest in football, only in the substantial profits.

The Department of Sport allocated approximately 1.000,000 euros annually for club maintenance and expenses related to league competition, coaching staff, cleaners, fire brigade, referees, game officials, player salaries, and travel costs for away games. However, once the funds were deposited into the club account, Boris instructed the club secretary to withdraw all the money from the bank account, leaving a balance of zero. The secretary was also an attorney by profession, and he was adept at managing funds discreetly.

Upon the funds being deposited into the account, Boris directed the secretary to collect all money and deliver them to him. Year after year, this pattern persisted. Funds continuously flowed into the club, yet they consistently vanished. The coaching staff was not compensated; they consisted of experienced, licensed coaches who had a profound passion for football.

They were apprehensive about complaining to Boris, hoping that he would someday choose to grant them their hard-earned salaries. All individuals employed at the club worked without compensation; Boris exploited his reputation to appropriate resources for himself while neglecting to settle any outstanding invoices.

The academy coaches volunteered their time out of a passion for football and a strong connection to the players. Boris understood their motivation but exploited it inappropriately to evade making any payments.

Despite the underlying mafia operations in the club, the coaches consistently developed high-quality players each year, prepared for the competitive demands of the football market.

The most exceptional players would sign contracts with the club, ensuring substantial financial returns from their future international transfers. Players such as Marko would enter into contracts with Boris, who would feign to be their protector in the pursuit of their childhood aspirations and eventual success.

The club where Marko and Nikola were raised sold approximately 30 players over a five-year period for a total of 20 million euros. The funds were solely deposited into Boris's account, where he utilized them to develop commercial properties, launder the money, and systematically reinvest it in legitimate enterprises, making it difficult to establish his liability in any context. Boris's sole motivation was to embezzle funds from the club, disregarding the welfare of the underpaid coaches, cleaners, and other staff members. Game fixing was just another source of income, in addition to player transfers and government-appointed funds.

Chapter 11
Learning the Lesson,
the Hard Way

After attending a party at the city nightclub, Marko was driving home with his girlfriend, Maria. At the time, he was driving his car at a speed of 200 kilometres per hour throughout the tinny streets in urban area. The car finally stopped.

As he parked in front of girlfriend's house, four police cars were surrounding him. Loud sirens sounded as multiple police officers rushed toward Marko's vehicle.

"Get off the vehicle and walk slowly, lowering your hands as you leave."

"Do not make any unnecessary movements; lie down on the road facing down," the police officer commanded Marko.

Marko was under the influence of cocaine at that time. His confusion about the entire situation grew stronger, and he was convinced that the event was just an illusion created by his own imagination. He closed his eyes, attempting to awaken from the troubling dream. However, it was not a dream; it was reality. Each small step and incorrect decision he made sequentially led him to this situation. He was breathing heavily while attempting to comprehend the situation.

The raindrops intensified with each passing second, and Marko pressed his lips against the cold asphalt. The police officer stepped with the dirty and muddy shoe on Marko's back.

As the police officer was placing handcuffs on Marko, he clarified, "You are under arrest for driving a stolen vehicle and for the drug possession discovered in the trunk. Also, you will have the opportunity to speak with your lawyer shortly."

Marko was arrested for operating a stolen vehicle.

That clarifies why Boris easily gave him that car. Additionally, the quantity of drugs located in the trunk of the vehicle was adding the serious trouble. It seemed that Marko's poor life choices appeared to have led him to significant trouble. He found himself incarcerated among notorious criminals, he felt frightened when the police escorted him to the prison cell that he shared with ten other inmates. That was the detention facility, where all inmates shared the space while awaiting their trials. The way other prisoners viewed Marko instilled a sense of fear for his life. Marko has not received any updates or information regarding his case for approximately three days when his brother Nikola visited him.

Upon the meeting, Marko was unable to contain his tears.

"I apologize, Nik; I should have heeded your advice. Had I listened your advice, the situation would have turned out differently. My career has come to an end, Nik."

"Shhhh. Please pay close attention, Marko. Do not disclose any information regarding the game fixing to anyone.

Do not tell to investigators the identity of the individual who provided you with that stolen vehicle, ok?

"An international police operation was conducted to locate thousands of vehicles that had been stolen in Germany and Switzerland and were subsequently imported here. Law enforcement seeks clarification regarding how the incident occurred."

Please pay attention; it is not too late. You need to trust me; there is still hope. I will ensure your release from this place ; please only be patient.

Nikola was holding Marko's clammy hand and gazing at him with the care of an older brother. Marko wept uncontrollably and was reluctant to release Nikola's hand. He felt scare.

"I apologize, Nik; I wish I had listen. I am filled with fear. The freaks in the cell are looking at me while muttering something strange at night; I am scared to sleep."

"Stay strong, Marko. The past is unchangeable. However, we can and must collaboratively shape the future. You and I against the world , do you remember our childhood game?

"You are my everything in this world. Now is the time to show your courage. You will be safe here; no one will harm you. I assure you that I will help you with everything. Just give me a few days."

I have communicated with our neighbour, Stevan, an older gentleman.

He has a deep affection for you and is willing to assist us. He assured me that he would provide you with the best lawyer, Marko. "Please remain strong; I must leave now."

Nikola exited the jail in tears.

Upon returning home, Nikola contacted his neighbour, Stevan. "I apologize for the call, sir; my brother is in trouble. He requires legal representation to secure his release from jail. I am becoming increasingly concerned for his well-being; he is not suited to thrive in a prison environment."

"Don't worry, my dear. I will do everything I can to assist; I will contact a lawyer friend of mine, and we will explore options to help Marko.

"He is a well-intentioned individual who has made some unwise choices in life. However, we can still rectify the situation; it is not too late, stay positive," the old man responded serenely.

Chapter 12
Difficulty to Adapt

Marko faced challenges in adapting to cruel jail system. He was bullied by older prisoners, seemingly without justification. He was targeted due to being an easy victim in the gritty, status-driven prison atmosphere.

In the coming days, Nikola will receive favourable news. One of the most experienced lawyers accepted Marko's case and committed to defending him. Certainly, a substantial fee was necessary for those services; however, their wealthy neighbour Stevan offered himself to manage those expenses. The issue arose from Marko being apprehended in a stolen vehicle, which contained drugs in the trunk. The police encouraged him to disclose the identity of the person who provided him with the car, but Marko declined, being concerned for his safety if he decided to talk.

After spending 30 days in jail, a police inspector visited Marko in prison.

The prison guard opened the clanging bars and summoned Marko. "Hello, you small, stinky rodent. Get your ass here; someone wishes to speak with you."

Marko walked slowly out of his cell and proceeded to the small room designated for visits.

"You look unwell, Marko. My name is Zdravko. I have observed several of your football matches, and I admire your dribbling skills and goal-scoring ability. Please know that I am here to help you, not to harm you. We can reach a favourable agreement with police, you may leave by tomorrow if you wish. I am confident in your innocence; we merely need to ask a few questions and document the statement.

"Do not be afraid, young man; I am here to support you," concluded police inspector Zdravko.

"Sir, with all due respect, you are all interconnected. It required several poor decisions for me to gain that understanding. You are wearing a police jacket, yet, perhaps you work for Boris? You came here to inquire if I will disclose anything about the drugs found in the car? Is that the actual reason for your visit? Who dispatched you here?" Marko suddenly raised his voice.

"I am conducting my own undercover investigation, boy. You must have trust in me. I have dedicated the past three months to collecting information and documents in order to build a case for the apprehension of numerous individuals engaged in unlawful activities.

"Do not judge me. Life is not always a matter of clear distinctions. Everything exists in a state of neutrality, represented by shades of grey. I recognize the reasons for your concern. However, the police department is not exclusively comprised of rigged people. The presence of good value in between contributes to an overall sense of balance in this world, boy. I am attempting to create a balance, but I require your assistance."

"What balance?" Marko inquired, surprised, and shook his head.

"The balance between good and evil. I take great pride in my work and consider it a privilege to assist citizens like you. I am committed to seeking justice and truth, and I fear no one." Zdravko stated.

Marko paused for a few seconds, before he kept talking.

"Please understand, you are wasting your time. I have concern about your trustworthiness. Do you really believe you can apprehend Boris? Are you aware of his connection and associations? Do you understand that he is shielded by high-ranking government officials? Are you informed that prominent police directors receive monthly compensation from Boris? Are you cognizant of the extent of his influence, Sir?"

Police inspector stood up from his chair in surprise at Marko's ability to clearly understand the entire system.

"I am aware, that is the reason for my visit today. I am not the only police officer performing my duties diligently and with pride, believe me. I have spent several months gathering information and preparing for significant arrests. Larger ocean fish can also be caught; only improved planning and stronger bait are required. I require extensive information, and I assure you that my operation will ultimately be successful. I acknowledge that Boris has significantly impacted the lives of many young athletes, including yourself, I understand your experience, but it is important for you to believe that I am here to support you."

Marko was unaffected after hearing this words.

"I am feeling exhausted, Zdravko…At my core, I desire to trust you and believe in your genuine intentions; however, it is challenging due to my experiences over the past few months. This individual is safeguarded from politicians in a manner akin to that of a polar bear. Because the government employs individuals like Boris for their questionable activities."

"Alright, here is a proposal. I will provide you with my phone number. I will be available for your call when you are ready to speak with me. I am here to ensure that other young football players do not follow the same path as you. I am collaboratively working with international law enforcement and certain prosecutors; any information you can provide would be greatly appreciated. Please feel free to contact me at your convenience; I am available to assist you. Stay strong, boy."

The police inspector Zdravko tapped Marko on the shoulder and exited the visitor room in the jail.

The days passed very slowly for Marko. His attorney attempted to establish Marko's innocence; however, the effort was challenging due to Marko's refusal to testify against Boris and his associates. Marko was apprehensive about doing that, even though police Inspector Zdravko assured him of his safety should he choose to speak up. This situation increased the complexity of the lawyer's responsibilities, and Marko remained in custody, awaiting hopeful updates.

Nikola's training routine remained unaffected by recent events. The level of commitment Nikola displayed was still strong. He participated in several trial games with various clubs, during which he was observed by several managers; however, none of them followed up with a response. One day, after exhausting training sessions, Nikola returned home. His cell phone rang just as he was about to take a cold bath, a routine part of his post-training regimen.

"Good afternoon. Am I speaking with Mr Nikola?"

Nikola still had to determine the identity of that individual.

"Indeed, it is me; how may I assist you, sir?"

"I am Ricardo, a football manager associated with a renowned and reputable Portuguese soccer agency. Several months ago, I went to various meetings in Serbia and unintentionally joined my fellow Serbians to watch your team's game. I had no intention of watching any games; my visit to your country served a different purpose. But I came to watch," he paused.

"And?!?" Nikola was nervous and eager to hear the continuation of the sentence.

"Well, you are an exceptional player. You were evaluated by my team for your gaming manoeuvres.

"It was an outstanding performance. The efficiency of passing, the speedy retrieval of possession for your team, and your precise, timely, yet enthralling tackles. Two excellent assists were given by you during the game, though. Nikola, I want to be straightforward with you. Perhaps, during that game, you experienced a wonderful, perfect match. You understand what I mean, those days when everything aligns perfectly in your favour and the minor details fall into place. I am just indicating a possibility. However, for me, that was sufficient to evoke a sense of wonder. Do you have a licensed manager representing you in the football market?"

"No, Mr Ricardo, I am currently unrepresented, without any clubs or managers.

"So, if you're okay, we'll give you a run-out shortly. Would you be interested?"

Nikola felt as if his heart would leap from his chest. His tongue and lips became numb. His mouth felt dry; he was attempting to remain calm, but was unable to do so. Probably due to the commitment he has been showing lately and the situation with his brother Marko.

"Nikola, are you present?" Ricardo inquired.

"Sir, I apologize; I am simply feeling a bit overwhelmed by everything." I am indeed interested in your offer. If I were to achieve that, it would be a fulfilment of my dreams.

Ricardo possessed well-established connections in both Portugal and Spain. He intended to send Nikola to trial matches for prestigious clubs.

Ricardo was a prominent agent in the football industry. He was renowned throughout the European continent for his talent recognition skills and his ability to uncover exceptional football potential. He observed Nikola without a specific scouting plan; it was a more unforeseen occurrence.

Nikola needed to get ready for his trial match in Portugal, Ricardo informed him that the game would occur in Lisbon in two weeks.

Nikola aimed to arrive in Portugal early to explore the area, start promptly, and prepare for the significant opportunity ahead. The paperwork, which included obtaining a Portugal visa and finding a place for Nikola in Lisbon, was managed by Ricardo. He also provided Nikola with some pocket money for the journey.

A few days later, Nikola was ready to depart.

He organized all his personal belongings and was eager to fully commit to the journey ahead.

On the flight to Lisbon, Nikola took a seat next to the window. As the plane prepared for take-off, Nikola experienced a blend of emotions; he felt both excited about this new chapter in his life and hopeful about the prospect of signing a professional contract with the club from the Portuguese league.

However, on the back of his mind, Nikola expressed concern for his brother Marko.

How does he cope with the challenges of life in prison? Is he resilient enough to overcome these circumstances?

To some extent, Nikola became more motivated. He wanted to be a successful football player in order to help his brother and rescue him from an unhealthy environment.

Chapter 13
Diamonds Never Crack
Under Pressure

Throughout the years, we gradually gain insight into our own emotions. The initial step in the learning process is to recognize those emotions.

The next step is to learn how to manage those emotions. Improvement in that area may require years or even decades. Once we have mastered these two fundamental components of emotional intelligence, we can progress to demonstrating compassion and empathy towards others. This capacity is what significantly impacts our personal lives and workplace environments. We must first analyse our behaviour to comprehend our environment and the individuals within it. Understanding others is a challenging endeavour, particularly when we do not first understand our own reactions and emotions. Effective listening skills are essential for enhancing one's ability to comprehend others. When someone speaks, we should actively participate and demonstrate that we value their input. This is how we earn lasting respect from those around us.

Upon mastering these three transformative skills, synergy with the broader world emerges effortlessly, akin to a cherry atop a beautifully crafted cake. By learning to identify and recognize our own emotions, managing those emotions, and demonstrating understanding and compassion towards others, we prepare ourselves to merge our energy and knowledge with the broader world, fostering synergy for the greater good.

The challenges Nikola faced were the unavoidable cost of achieving his legacy: the greater the ambitions, the more substantial the hurdles. The action of standing up to criminal Boris was like being in a cage with 100 hungry hyenas. Nikola has always preferred lions over hyenas. The two animals are hunters; yet the lions have something that they can't match, and it's their majestic roar with determination to win in every encounter.

Nikola's call for his brother's justice served as a warning that ravenous hyenas were approaching. Lions may occasionally face superior numbers, yet they refuse to retreat, regardless of how many hungry hyenas approach.

Chapter 14
Arrival in Portugal

The plane arrived in Lisbon. A member of the Ricardo team met Nikola at the airport arrival area and drove him to a nearby hotel. Nikola had several days remaining to prepare for the friendly match organized for potential new signings of Fc Sporting Club.

Upon arrival, Nikola placed his baggage in the hotel room and chose to go for a low-intensity jog to explore the surrounding area. The stadium of Sporting FC is situated approximately 4 km from the hotel where Nikola was residing. Light jogging to stretch his legs after the 2-hour flight proved to be effective.

He recognized that the intense and demanding training sessions he had undertaken for several months would yield beneficial results. Nikola chose to have faith in himself and was determined to realize his dream.

When the opportunity arises, it is too late to prepare. You must be prepared for that moment and willing to overcome any obstacles in your way.

On the second day, when Nikola arrived, his agent Ricardo visited him and took him for lunch at a nearby restaurant.

"How are you feeling, Nikola? Are you ready for the game? You still have a few days to acclimate to the weather, food, and environment, and to prepare your body for optimal performance."

"Thank you, Mr Ricardo; I am ready. I was prepared, sir. My brother is facing significant difficulties in Serbia. He is all that I currently have in this world. I am concerned that something negative may occur to him."

Nikola started to open up about his personal problems.

"Oh, Nikola…I understand that your affection for your brother makes it challenging to concentrate fully. However, it is essential that you take this action for him; this presents an opportunity to help your entire family. This is a unique opportunity of a lifetime. I have communicated with the manager of FC Sporting; he will attend to observe you and the club representatives. I informed them that you have a special talent.

"It is advisable to concentrate on recreating that level of performance, that is crucial for your future football career. I understand that it is challenging to perform under significant pressure; however, that is a part of life, my boy. Are you aware of the distinction between regular brick and diamond, Nikola?"

"What do you mean by brick and diamond, sir? I don't understand," Nikola responded, visibly perplexed.

"Both brick and diamond belong to the same category of rocks. The sole distinction lies in their responses to pressure. It will fracture if extreme pressure is applied to the small brick. On the other side, putting significant physical pressure on the diamond will not cause it to crack, but it will become brighter. This game presents you with an opportunity to excel under pressure, young man. In the future, if everything appears perfect in your life, pause on the street, take off your shoe, place a small rock inside, and then proceed with your walk. The minor discomfort caused by the small stone in your shoe will ultimately become your ally. It will keep you alert, attentive, and eager."

"Sir, I have a clear understanding of your point. That is motivating story. I am committed to meeting your requirements, and I am aware that several important individuals will be attending to observe my performance. The sole reason for their attendance to watch me is their trust in your word and recommendation. I will not disappoint you, sir."

"Understood, Nikola. Make sure to get adequate rest and prepare yourself both mentally and physically. The game is in four days. Let's do this together."

Chapter 15
Emotional Struggle

Four days remaining. Nikola struggled to sleep that night following a discussion with Ricardo. He was extremely enthusiastic and eager. If only he could press a button to accelerate time. The significant concern regarding his brother Marko was foremost in Nikola's thoughts. How is he faring in jail?

Can he withstand the pressure and stay resilient? When will he have the opportunity to see his brother again?

The questions raced through his mind with lightning speed. Although his eyes were closed, he was unable to fall asleep. His heart raced as he rose from the bed and began to pace around the room. It was approximately 2:00 AM. Nikola approached the window of the hotel room.

With soft and delicate steps, he drew the curtain to the side. While Nikola observed the streetlight's brightness, he also saw several people hugging and singing in Portuguese. Nikola observed those individuals until they turned around the corner.

There was a tear drop that went down the window's metal base. Nikola intended to erase it and used the palm of his hand to grasp the tiers gently.

He felt the absence of his mother and father. This important game was approaching, yet he felt isolated, lacking anyone to share his enthusiasm.

Moreover, he couldn't stop thinking about his brother. What is he doing at this hour? Is he safe? Is he able to sleep at all?

Nikola felt a sense of emptiness at that moment. Throughout his life, he had been eagerly anticipating this moment, but now a feeling of incompleteness prevailed over him. He felt a sense of sadness because the moment held significant importance, yet also seemed trivial. He would exchange the football game, his career, wealth, fame, luxury vehicles, and house for the safety and freedom of his brother Marko, if it were possible.

Throughout the night, Nikola was restless in bed.

The following day, Nikola awoke late; it was already 1PM. He quickly got out of bed and jumped to his phone to call his neighbour, Stevan. He wished to inquire if there had been any updates regarding Marko's situation in jail.

"Good afternoon, Mr Stevan. How are you? I intended to ask you…"

"There's no need to be concerned about your brother," Stevan interjected before Nikola could complete his thought.

"I visited your brother yesterday with the lawyer. The lawyer is a close friend of mine and a leading expert in his field. He will look after your brother."

"Thank you, Mr Stevan; I feel more at ease now. I was sick and worried; Marko is not suited for prison."

"I understand, Nikola; it is natural for you to be worried. However, he is your older brother. He has reached the age of being able to provide self-care. We are all making every effort to assist him. In addition to all of that, it is essential to concentrate on your performance. This is a unique opportunity of a lifetime. It is advisable to worry less, conserve your energy, and stay focused. I have faith in you, young man!"

"Thank you, Mr Stevan. I will contact you after my game. Please extend my greetings to Marko. He does not have a phone, so I am unable to reach him."

"I will. Please remain resilient, Nik."

The following day, his agent Ricardo picked him up in front of the hotel. The journey to Sporting FC's stadium was brief. As they entered the stadium grounds, Nikola carefully took in every detail, savouring the experience of being present in that moment.

The head coach of Sporting Lisbon approached the dressing room and greeted Nikola, introducing himself in a friendly manner.

"Mr Ricardo spoke highly of your qualities and exceptional athletic abilities in running. I've been informed that you have the ability to cover a significant amount of ground and display great effectiveness with the ball. Today, try to occupy yourself with some relaxation and enjoyment on the field. We will be competing in a friendly match against Nica, a team from French Ligue 1."

Although Nikola acquired English language skills in high school, he lacked opportunities to utilize or enhance them through practice. Nikola acknowledged his understanding of the coach's instructions by smiling at Coach Tite instead of verbally responding.

Shortly after, Nikola entered the dressing room. All of his teammates greeted him with high fives before the game, making him feel welcomed despite not knowing any of them. The typical duration of the warm-up session was 25 minutes.

Nikola experienced a slight feeling of tension, yet remained firmly focused. The game commenced, with Nikola positioned in the central midfield area of the field. From the moment, the referee's whistle signalled the start of the game,

Nikola dashed forward with urgency and determination. Upon receiving the ball at his feet, he made a conscious effort to play accurate, progressive passes.

In this manner, Nikola would experience a boost in confidence and performance as the game unfolds.

Throughout the game, Nikola achieved a 93% success rate in passing, won 8 out of 10 tackles, prevailed in 4 out of 5 aerial duels, covered a total distance of 10. 8 km, created four key opportunities for his teammates, and provided an impressive assist for the winning goal.

On that particular day, he delivered the most outstanding performance of his life. Nikola approached that game with a heightened sense of motivation. At the sound of the referee's final whistle, Sporting FC emerged victorious with a 2-1 win, with Nikola performing exceptionally well. As he made his way to the dressing room, he was filled with joy as he received warm greetings from both the coach and his teammates. Nikola was confident that his dedication and hard work had sufficiently prepared him for this day, optimistic that it would secure the signing of the contract.

After showering, as he prepared to exit the dressing room, his agent Ricardo appeared with a beaming smile.

"Nikola, come here! We did it! They are thrilled with your talents and have offered us a contract with Sporting Fc! You've made it, son!" Ricardo exclaimed excitedly.

Overwhelmed, Nikola grabbed his shirt and knelt down. He was chuckling and beaming simultaneously. Is there such a thing as a fairy tale ending in real life? He found it hard to comprehend. Despite facing numerous challenges, he managed to reach the pinnacle of success!

Few days after, Nikola secured a lucrative four-year deal with Sporting FC valued at 4,000,000 euros. He was set to receive approximately 1 million per year in addition to bonuses.

Chapter 16
Importance of Planting the Quality Seeds

The seeds we sow will determine the harvest we reap. Amidst this period, Marko endured a distressing ordeal while being locked in jail. He endured imprisonment, abuse, and repeated physical assaults to his face over the course of several months. His lawyer was diligently working to secure his freedom. Yet, successfully completing this task proved challenging due to the gravity of the charges related to drug possession and car theft.

While waiting in line for his meal, Marko was approached by several inmates one day. "Are you feeling hungry, young man? The tax for territory within the jail is a matter of great importance. Have you presumed that this food is complimentary? Kindly provide the payment, boy"—a member of the group approached Marko as he was preparing to set his plate down at the table.

He was encircled by four senior inmates, older criminals. Marko attempted to locate the police guard, but found no one in the vicinity. He was tasked with handling the elderly individuals on his own.

They continuously raised their voices at Marko, questioning his understanding of their language and insinuating that he was feigning deafness.

At one point, one of them menacingly brandished a pocket knife and directed it towards Marko.

Marko remained composed despite his youth and challenging circumstances.

Instead of panicking, he calmly observed a bird flying outside through the small window of the jail. Currently, the bird represents freedom, the opportunity to fly once again and reach new heights. No one directed the bird's flight path or restricted its movements. Marko was mesmerized by the stunning green and blue wings of the bird. He had chosen to focus on the bird soaring towards freedom and eternity, rather than the knife pointed menacingly at him.

Abruptly, the individual wielding the knife issued a final warning. "Give me your money you little bastard, or I will harm you badly!"

Marko confidently raised his head to face the criminal in the eyes.

Without anyone knowing, Marko secretly noticed the knife position, that was lying near his navel. With determination, Marko grasped the knife with his left hand and dropped it to ground. Using his right hand, he delivered a powerful right hook directly to the jaw of the criminal facing him. The strike was effective, causing the criminal to fall to the ground.

Marko was immediately overwhelmed by the sudden attack from the other group members. He found himself in the minority, yet a sense of unwavering resilience emanated from his heart. He was prepared to face death in that instant.

When faced with 20 hyenas in pursuit, the courageous lion does not retreat but rather upholds his principles by defending his independence and honour through confrontation.

Despite being outnumbered, his resilient fighting spirit remained undefeated. He took some nasty hits to his head and a brutal kicks to the stomach, yet he stood his ground.

Just prior to authorities intervening in the altercation, Marko seized a metal chair from the kitchen and forcefully struck a gang member in the face. The police escorted him to the side and proceeded to separate the individuals.

"Your fate is sealed, young lad. It's impossible to find a place to hide." "It's over for you," exclaimed the gang member who were shouting at Marko.

The police officer alerted his colleague, indicating the wound on Marko's stomach where he was bleeding. Despite the adrenaline and intense fight, Marko did not initially realize he had been stabbed until the knife fell to the ground. There was a noticeable bleed coming from the left side of his stomach. The two officers quickly transported him to the prison hospital.

Fortunately, upon arrival, it was determined that Marko did not have any injuries that posed a threat to his life. Upon thorough evaluation, it was determined that he had sustained a minor cut on the left side of his abdomen. Fortunately, there was no injury to any critical organs, and the damage to his arteries and veins was minimal.

Marko remained in a stable and conscious state. The individuals involved in the assault were notorious for their history of violent attacks on numerous inmates. An attempt was made to instil fear in the other prisoners in order to extort money from them, but Marko stood firm.

The gang member suffered a brain concussion during the altercation.

After a few hours, the jail director paid a visit to Marko as he recuperated from his injuries.

"How are you, young man? I am aware of the circumstances that led to your presence in this facility, and I understand that you are not a criminal. I am also aware that you will be departing from this location in two weeks. Avoid getting into any more trouble, as I am aware of the recent attack on you by other individuals. It is fortunate that you have survived.

"For your safety, I will isolate you in a single cell for the next two weeks. Your attorney and the judge have reached an agreement for your release in approximately two weeks."

"Single-cell, how will I manage in there, sir?"

"Do not be concerned. It is in your best interest for things to be as they are. My duty as the manager of this jail is to ensure your safety without any risk. Due to recent events, individuals with whom you are in disagreement. It is advisable to avoid contact with them for the upcoming two weeks. Every day for the next 14 days, you'll receive food from the guard in your lone cell. That concludes the explanation. Ensure your well-being, young man," the jail director left the scene.

Marko experienced a sense of joy in that instant. In two weeks, he will regain his freedom, much like the bird he glimpsed through the window earlier that day. Following a two-day stay in the prison hospital, Marko was transferred to his new solitary confinement cell. The cell had a modest size, slightly larger than a standard shoe box, measuring approximately three square meters. In one corner of the room, there was a small toilet, surrounded by an old, musty mattresses covered in dust and mould.

Marko was nearing freedom, but the most difficult days still lay ahead. The cells were designated for the most notorious offenders—those who had broken laws, attacked police officers, or engaged in domestic violence within the prison. Lack of windows presented a challenge to survival in this prison cell. Even the addition of a small window would have a significant impact, enhancing the overall appearance and functionality. In this place, it could hold even 'hard-core' people off.

Marko received three daily meals from the police guard, who would unlock the small cage, slide the plate of food inside, and secure it once more. Marko refrained from eating for the initial 24 hours, and he carefully monitored every inch of the place. Mold had developed on the green stain of the jail wall, and it smelled bad—combined with the smell of nearby lavatory. It seemed like the toilet had not been cleaned in recent times. Marko found it nearly impossible to eat with that smell lingering in the air. He waited a mere 48 hours before taking his first bite of food after being confined to the solitary prison cell. There was a complete absence of sound and light in the surroundings. Visitation was prohibited for all inmates confined to the individual prison cell. Marko's character and personality were truly put to the test by the crazy living conditions.

He was unaware of the time of day due to the absence of light. He did not know if it was 3:00 pm or 11:00 am. He was unable to perceive any external noise from his current location. He struggled with sleeping at night due to his uncertainty about the time of day.

The rigorous challenge of self-resilience proved overwhelming for a young, inexperienced boy. After three days in that state, Marko began doing push ups to get his body back into shape. He became accustomed to breathing in unpleasant odours, and exercising helped to clear his mind of excessive contemplation.

After completing his meal, he would neatly place the plate in the corner. At night, as he reclined on the mattress, the only noise disturbing his rest was the sound of the nearby laundry within its foundation. From the corridor nearby, a dim light shone into the small corner of the prison cell. Marko would station himself in a small corner to catch a glimpse of the faint light emanating from the jail corridor. The glimmer of hope he experienced was crucial to preventing a rapid mental breakdown in the absence of light.

Throughout the night, he would fixate his gaze on a specific spot in the ceiling. He found solace in the knowledge that, even amidst challenging circumstances, there remained a flicker of hope for what lay ahead. He reminisced on pleasant childhood memories shared with Nikola. Recreating beautiful childhood memories imbued him with a sense of purpose in his life.

Marko was making an effort to focus on positive memories and maintain an optimistic outlook on life. He resolved not to dwell on past mistakes and circumstances that brought him to his current situation, feeling trapped like an animal. He understood that succumbing to these emotions would not be appropriate, given the already complex and challenging nature of his surroundings. Attributing blame to himself would only exacerbate the situation and diminish his strength. While all of this was not supposed to happen, Marko found himself unable to change his past.

He acknowledged the cost involved and was open to gaining insights from the unavoidable circumstance. It is common to feel responsible when faced with setbacks, yet each experience should be seen as an opportunity for growth and learning. Occasionally, the reasons behind unfolding events become clear, while other times, it may take years or even a decade to understand the necessity of certain occurrences.

After spending nearly six months incarcerated, Marko was compelled to mature and assume the responsibilities of adulthood. From a person who was overly self-important and had values that were no match for his own, Marko learned valuable lessons that helped him become much more mature. Life imparted a lasting lesson to him through a series of challenges and also stripped away Marko's freedom, ultimately strengthening his resilience and compelling him to unearth his hidden inner strength in order to endure the harsh conditions of the notorious jail.

Chapter 17
Freedom as a Sense of Hope

Marko suddenly heard footsteps, hinting at a glimmer of hope ahead. It seemed as if the heavy police booths were splitting the silence of the prison corridor with their loud sound. A man with a deep, gravelly voice approached the prison cell and commanded in a loud tone, "Step out, young man. It's time to leave and get ready for your journey home." Marko stood up from his bed, uncertain if he was dreaming or if this was reality.

For about two weeks, Marko has been waiting with anticipation to speak with someone else. Additionally, he needed to ascertain the day and time as a result of the absence of natural light in his prison cell.

"Did you hear me, young man? Will you stay here or come with me? The question from the police guard made Marko's mind go blank. Yes, sir, I will exit; please give me a moment," Marko responded.

Having refrained from bathing for approximately two weeks, Marko also experienced significant weight loss during his confinement.

Gradually, Marko exited the facility alongside the police guard. They visited the room to retrieve Marko's personal belongings and complete the necessary paperwork.

It was a Sunday. Marko recognized that it was the perfect opportunity to visit his former club to watch the game and reconnect with his old friends. He also intended to request that the club secretary release his registration and documents. When he approached the stadium, he felt a sense of unease. He experienced a sense of insecurity and pressure in his chest. As he descended the stairs towards the club's main entrance, a few teammates spotted him.

"Marko! You're back, brother; it's wonderful to see you with us again."

"Hi, boys, it has been a while. I miss all of you; you truly are a wonderful group of people. I will be cheering for you from the stands today! Win this game for me! Marko expressed his heartfelt emotions to his teammates."

As Marko was about to take a seat, someone shouted from behind…

"Look who's back, our young talented footballer who chose a life of crime."

Marko immediately recognized that voice. It was the club president, Boris.

"Good day, sir; I was attempting to…" Marko began to speak, but Boris swiftly interrupted him.

"You don't need to say anything, boy. I only needed to clarify information about the character you have displayed since the arrest. Yet, you made a courageous and prudent choice to refrain from speaking to the police officers. By doing so, you safeguarded me, and I appreciate individuals who are discreet.

"In my business, I will refrain from providing any information to the police, even if I am arrested.

"It is the code of conduct within our industry, understood, gentlemen? What I appreciate about you, young man, is that you could secure your release immediately after being arrested if you chose to provide the police with some information regarding me.

"Nonetheless, you made a commendable decision; I can assure you of that," Boris concluded his remarks.

"Certainly, sir, I would never inconvenience you or anyone else." I prefer not to betray others. Anyway, Sir, I wanted to ask you something, if that's alright...

Marko inched closer to his main question.

"Yes, anything; go ahead," Boris replied while holding the large Cuban cigar.

"I wanted to have my papers released. I would like to obtain all the documents, as I may consider transferring to another club. It has certainly been some time since I last trained. Nonetheless, I would like to inquire whether it is permissible to have my papers released?"

Boris extinguishes his cigar on the nearby fence. He took off his glasses and stepped closer to Marko.

"Yes, Marko. Certainly. I enjoy assisting others. I am a generous person, and I believe that helping others is a valuable endeavour. However, I dedicated significant time and effort to the development of this club. I completely understand that it is only natural for you to depart now.

"However, there seems to be something suspicious about this situation. Why do you want your papers? Aren't you excited to return and play for our club? I still have significant plans for your future."

"Sir, I genuinely want to leave. This is my definitive decision. I have personal reasons for needing my papers to be released."

"Please listen to me, Marko. If I were malicious, I would now demand 100,000 euros for your documents. It is just purely business. If someone requests your releasing contract, I will inform them that there is a specific fee required. I want to be fair to you because you are a good person and much smarter than your brother.

"Therefore, here is my final offer to you: I will require your presence in the squad next week, as we have a pre-scheduled game coming up. The owner of the opposing club is my business partner, and we have a significant agreement for next week's game..."

Marko interrupted Boris with a bewildered expression.

"But sir, I haven't trained in nearly seven months; I was in jail and I'm not fit to play!"

"That's precisely what I need, boy. Players who are unfit or of low calibre. Do you comprehend that our objective is to ensure we lose that game? Additionally, please refrain from discussing this matter. You are scheduled to participate in the game next Sunday, and after the game is finished, I will provide you with your documents and release papers. Win-win, you benefit, and so do I, do you understand?"

"I suppose I have no choice but to agree?" Marko replied with a grimace.

"No, Marko. You have an option, my boy. We all do. However, it is important to recognize that you can only acquire something if you are prepared to make a payment. At times, we compensate for it with our finances, time, or other resources. Some individuals even pay with their lives, do you understand?"

Marko stood frozen when he heard that final sentence from Boris. Is he being cautioned to accept and participate in the rigged game? Does he have the option to decline? These questions raced through his mind.

"Okay, sir. I will play the game next weekend."

"That's a good boy," Boris said, tapping him on the shoulder.

"You have made a wise choice. Remember, that game is designed for us to lose; refrain from attempting to score or be overly clever. The directive is clear: we will lose the game. After that, you will receive your documents."

Chapter 18
Mafia Transactions

Boris was never particularly interested in football as a sport. He was solely interested in the financial gains associated with it. Individuals like him benefitted from the protection of corrupt politicians and law enforcement officials. Boris was systematically organizing the outcomes of his club's games, generating a profitable income. The game-fixing cycle was closely linked to the owners of the betting companies. Everyone was pleased and enjoying their piece of cake.

Marko could hardly believe how complicated his life had become. From a young and talented player showing early signs of a promising career, he became an ex-prisoner involved in fixed games. His unreliable and erratic personality placed him in a challenging situation. Should he call his brother for advice? No, Nikola would simply become angry and disappointed because Marko chose to meet with Boris again. Instead, Marko chose to participate in one final fixed game for his former club to obtain his papers and registration documents before leaving the country.

During this period, the football landscape was rife with corruption, with individuals exploiting the sport to engage in unethical practices for personal gain. Individuals like Boris exploited the murky, low visibility system to secure their financial success regardless of the consequences. They employed harsh tactics to instil fear, inflict abuse, abduct, and torture individuals in order to gain respect and build their reputation. The social system represented a swollen bubble characterized by inappropriate values for the younger generation.

Many young teenagers admired Boris, viewing him as a symbol of success and the possibility of achieving everything without significant effort. The core values of fairness, hard work, and dignity lacked depth.

The government only aimed to promote patriotism among young people as a means to manipulate perceptions and divert attention from their unlawful activities. Several courageous and diligent journalists attempting to probe the covert ties between the government and the football mafia have gone missing. Their disappearance served as a warning to others seeking truth and justice, discouraging them from taking public action.

For Boris, the income derived from drug dealing was more perilous than obtaining significantly greater and easier profits in the football industry. Particularly due to his reputation, no one would dare to confront him or attempt to apprehend him. The government safeguarded him like a polar bear due to his role among the individuals operating behind the scenes in the country.

In contrast, football players and coaches became collateral damage in the pursuit of the selfish ambitions of individuals like Boris. The position of football coach was regarded as the most undervalued occupation in the country.

In the club where Boris served as president, coach Lazar held the highest coaching license. He was committed to his role, striving for continuous personal improvement each year. He focused on enhancing his coaching skills and devoted significant time and energy to developing numerous professional players. Lazar was also a father of three young children. As a football coach, he did not have any social insurance, a pension plan, and no salary package.

Individuals such as Boris exerted influence over him and the coaches of other teams. The government would officially allocate a significant sum of money to be distributed among the clubs, ensuring that family-oriented, respectable individuals like coach Lazar receive their well-deserved compensation.

The issue was that the corrupt system enabled Boris and other criminals to withdraw substantial sums of money from the club account without any legal restraints or repercussions. Coaches seldom receive competitive compensation. The individuals who will receive higher compensation are the coaches involved in game-fixing and closely associated with criminals like Boris. It required considerable effort to adhere to your core principles and strong values, or to settle for a small piece of the pie while sacrificing restful nights. Most coaches had no choice; they had to provide for their families at any cost. Life does not wait for anyone; bills must be settled, and food needs to be provided for Lazar's children.

Chapter 19
One Final Task to Be Complete

The day after speaking with the criminal Boris, Marko arrived for training session.

Marko felt revitalized. It has been some time since he last struck the ball, yet it was evident that he still possessed his skilled footwork. He thoroughly enjoyed himself and scored goals effortlessly during his first training session after a long time.

After the session, coach Lazar approached Marko.

"I can see you still have it, boy. Those were moves from another planet, Marko."

"Thank you, sir. I have missed engaging in my passion. Nothing else matters to me when I am playing football."

"That's wonderful, Marko; I am pleased for you."

"Listen kid…"

Coach Lazar paused and glanced down at the small butterfly that had settled on his foot.

Lazar smiled and proceeded in an unforeseen direction. "Butterflies are exquisite. It is truly remarkable. They are free to go wherever they choose, Marko. Observe the courage of this butterfly; it seems unafraid of my presence.

"Are you aware of what is intriguing about butterflies, Marko?" Coach Lazar lifted his gaze, giving Marko a mysterious and profound look.

"No, sir."

"Interestingly, they live only for one day. The butterflies undergo a stunning transformation in a brief period. They emerged as these beautiful, striking beings from the unpleasant warmth. They soar and radiate their beauty to everyone nearby, if only for a single day. They do not express dissatisfaction regarding their brief existence. Instead, butterflies are utilizing their allotted time in a uniquely special manner. They cherish and relish their freedom while it lasts, and then they meet their end."

"That is eloquently articulated, sir," Marko replied, taken aback by his coach.

"You see, Marko, I too long for the freedom of that butterfly," Lazar remarked as they watched the butterfly gracefully soar away, displaying its stunning wings.

"But sir, you have the freedom to do as you please, don't you?" Marko sought clarification.

"It's a complex question to answer. However, there are times when we must take necessary actions.

"Anyway, next weekend…we need to lose the game, understood?"

"Yes, sir." However, that is a considerate shock for me. Sports are intended to foster a positive set of values. I prefer not to be involved in that, boss. It is challenging for me because it is necessary for me to get my papers released by the club.

"Listen, Marko. You are an exceptionally skilled player and an intelligent young man. I recommend that you consider going to a location far from here. This living environment is significantly compromised. You either adapt to it, or it will consume you. There is nothing you can alter; it is as it stands, Marko. You need to seek out a new environment where your true value is recognized and appreciated. A nurturing environment is ideal for your transformation into a beautiful butterfly. Do you grasp my perspective? You need to seek an environment that fosters your growth and allows you to excel," Coach Lazar continued.

"Indeed, sir, it is challenging to thrive here without adaptation, but adapting often entails sacrificing our uniqueness and valuable traits. If I were to make a choice, I would prefer not to remain here any longer; I have endured more than enough in this country."

"Are you familiar with 'crab mentality', Marko?"

"No, sir, I am not," Marko responded attentively.

"If you observe hundreds of crabs in a large bucket, you will notice that some are attempting to climb to the top in pursuit of freedom. Simultaneously, crabs at the bottom of the bucket are attempting to pull down those that are rising. The crabs at the bottom are not concerned with seeking freedom; their sole focus is on pulling back any crabs attempting to escape the bucket. The situation is similar in this country, particularly within the football industry. This is merely a small bucket, Marko. Most individuals in your environment may not support your desire to rise above this situation; instead, they may attempt to hold you back. They lack the courage to attempt to escape from this bucket independently. They are envious of your courage, strength, dignity, and determination to stand up. They prefer you to remain in the mud because they cannot handle your escape from the bucket.

Therefore, it is essential for you to be strong, Marko. You must exert yourself, invest all your energy, and break free from that bucket while you have the chance! You are capable of this, Marko!" coach Lazar concluded his inspiring and fervent guidance.

Marko was taken aback by his coach's motivational prowess. Every word resonated in his mind; he realized he had no time to waste; the escape from the bucket needed to commence at once.

Chapter 20
Happy Childhood Memories

Marko reminisced about the carefree days spent with Nikola in elementary school. At that time, they were not required to make major life decisions. They had no reason to be concerned about life. Their sole responsibility at that time was to engage in play throughout the day and experience genuine happiness. Marko reflected on how life had become too complicated.

Should he inform his brother? Should he contact Nikola for advice? A part of him felt inclined to do so, yet deep down, Marko could envision Nikola's reaction to this situation.

Marko was unsure whether he should participate in this fixed game solely to obtain his papers and registration documents. Having registration papers would facilitate the process of playing football elsewhere, along with clearance from his former club.

As he strolled along, Marko nostalgically revisited his former elementary school, reliving the joyous memories of his childhood. On a beautiful, sunlit autumn day, Marko brought along his worn football as he embarked on a 30-minute stroll to reach his elementary school.

Upon his arrival, three children were engaged in a game of ball on the concrete soccer field.

Marko attentively watched as the children chatted loudly, with delighted expressions evident on their faces. The children appeared to be the happiest in the world.

As Marko observed, a boy approached him and asked, "Would you like to join us in a game? There are three of us here, needing one more player for a two-against-two match on the small goals." Will you be joining us?

Marko experienced a brief moment of confusion. His face lit up with a joyful smile as he exclaimed: Absolutely, I would be delighted to join your game. It sounds like a lot of fun.

"Who is my playing partner? Who is my teammate?"

"He is the least skilled player among the others. You can play with him to ensure a fair game," the boy gestured towards his significantly smaller friend.

The game commenced, and Marko wore a smile that had not graced his face in quite some time. The young children, possibly around 10 or 11 years of age, displayed a strong sense of competitiveness, they ran after Marko, trying to steal the ball. According to the designated rule, if one team reach up five scored goals, then they will win.

The playing field featured two small goals delineated by large bricks, contributing to a tense and competitive game.

The score tied at 4-4.

"The next goal determines the winner; all or nothing!" Marko's teammate urged him loudly,

"Sir, pass me the ball, I'm open!" Suddenly, he experiences a moment of bliss as he realizes that happiness has returned. He had never experienced such a profound sense of happiness during his years of participating in competitive games.

Marko executed a stylish pass to his teammate in a moment of skill. His teammate, the little boy, successfully took the shot and secured the winning goal, eliciting an overwhelming sense of joy on the boy's face.

Running towards Marko, he leaped and shouted with excitement.

Following their victory, Marko approached the boy who was responsible for choosing the teams prior to the game.

"Did you label him as the least talented among you all?" Marko pointed at the victorious goal scorer.

The boy replied with a shameful answer, "Yes, sir," and instantly looked away from the situation.

"Now you understand the error of your judgement." When I was younger, everyone acknowledged that I possessed more talent than my brother. The manner in which I achieved the goals and other accomplishments.

Nikola paused for emphasis, ensuring everyone was attentive as they began to speak.

"Today…" "My brother is a member of one of the top football clubs in Europe, while I am currently not part of any team. That decision was mine, you see? Talent alone is not the determining factor; rather, it is the dedication, diligence, and passion invested that truly counts. This principle is not limited to football, but applicable to all aspects of life. Like a water-deprived flower, talent dies with no nourishment. Without water, even the most stunning flower will not be able to grow. All of you kids possess immense talent and radiate beauty. The key differentiator is your commitment to working diligently and improving consistently each day; your focus is solely on personal growth, rather than comparing yourself to others."

Marko presented his teammate with a gift: a ball to commemorate the winning goal. As he walked away, the boys watched, their smiles reflecting gratitude and admiration. As he distanced himself from the school, he glanced back one last time to see them still watching him, waving goodbye.

Chapter 21
Tough Call to Make

Marko made a decisive choice the following day. As part of an agreement to have his documents released, he will compete in his final match.

In this manner, he would have the freedom to register for any other club and reunite with his brother, Nikola, in Lisbon. Preparing extensively for his upcoming game seemed unnecessary, yet Marko maintained a disciplined routine of morning jogs followed by ball training. He also dedicated time to practicing free-kicks. Marko consistently remained tight-lipped about his strategy to secure the release of his documents through a rigged game whenever Nikola reached out to him. Nikola remained uninformed as Marko foresaw his likely reaction and advice.

Marko made an early appearance at the stadium, reflecting on his decision and whether it was morally justified.

He simply sought happiness and a return to playing football, away from his familiar surroundings.

To achieve this, he knew he had to participate in one final game and be involved in a customary match-fixing scenario. Numerous strategies were implemented to guarantee the successful execution of game fixing. Referees and select players from both teams would determine the outcome of certain pre-arranged games. The situation has undergone a transformation at present. The recommendation from coach Lazar was to bench the best players from his club, and to play junior players and Marko, who had been absent from team training for nine months.

With the formidable strength of the opponent in mind, Coach Lazar knew that fielding his most talented players would result in a challenging, evenly matched game in terms of predicting the final score. The intention was to utilize reserve players and potentially some members of the U19 squad in the game plan.

During the team's warm-up, Marko overheard the junior members eagerly discussing their determination to prove their worth by winning the upcoming game. Unbeknownst to them, these young and inexperienced football players were unaware that the match had already been prearranged. They remained determined to compete and achieve victory.

Once the game commenced, a marked disparity in quality was quickly evident on the field. Coach Lazar chose to take a more observant approach rather than giving direct instructions to his players. He watched closely as the opponent capitalized on multiple early opportunities to score, demonstrating a strong offensive presence on the field. The Marko team's goalkeeper, a teenager, made his professional league debut playing for the senior team for the very first time. He was aware of the situation and therefore continued to exert maximum effort in order to impress with his performance. Despite circumstances, he made 10 remarkable saves, holding the score at 0-0 going into halftime.

The opposing team squandered numerous excellent opportunities, striking the post twice and the crossbar once.

While watching, Boris was accompanied by the president of their opposing team. They diligently observed the developments on the field to ensure that the game result aligned with the predetermined strategy. There was a significant amount of money at stake in the game, with millions of euros being wagered.

During halftime, a hush fell over the dressing room as Marko entered. Out of nowhere, akin to lightning splitting the sky, the goalkeeper addressed his youthful teammates.

"Let's take a step forward, men. The first half was lacking energy and intensity. You abandoned me on the front line without offering support! I don't think this is fair! Let's put in extra effort in the second half," he declared as he paced, observing the expressions of those around him.

Marko remained silent. He experienced immense guilt, as if he had let down the young boy who once aspired to become a professional football player. Marko reflected on his extensive football career, encompassing countless hours of rigorous training and ultimately culminating in participation in rigged matches.

For what reason, just for a single document he required? With each passing minute, Marko grew increasingly infuriated with himself.

This behaviour was uncharacteristic of him; he could not continue to be associated with this scandal. The referee signalled the end of the first half with a whistle and the second half began. The opening of the second half mirrored the pattern of the entire first half. Marko struggled to gain possession of the ball as the opponent dominated possession and generated numerous scoring opportunities.

Surprisingly, the opponent failed to capitalize on the golden opportunities, with only 20 minutes remaining in the game and the score still tied at 0-0.

Club president Boris anxiously rose from his seat in the VIP section, reaching for his cell phone to contact coach Lazar.

The urgent message on the other end instructed him to make a strategic substitution if he wished to stay alive beyond the game. "Take immediate action!" Boris yelled angrily at coach Lazar.

Without any other choice, Lazar called the 18-year-old substitute goalkeeper, who appeared noticeably overweight. He had not previously played even for the U19 team, but now he was preparing for his debut at a professional football match.

Despite the starting goalkeeper's impressive performance, Marko' teammates were confused by the substitution. Marko was unsurprised, as he was aware of the situation at hand.

In the following moment, the new goalkeeper entered the game and promptly tripped an opposing player in the penalty box, resulting in an immediate penalty call from the referee. Penalty taking was momentarily postponed due to a player sustaining an injury on the pitch, prompting the doctor to intervene. Boris, seated in the stands, finally smiled.

He retrieved his phone from his pocket and made a second call to coach Lazar. "Please ask the goalkeeper to come over to the bench right away," he said. Instruct him to maintain position in the centre of the goal and refrain from trying to block the penalty shot.

"Are you able to comprehend my words?" At that instant, coach Lazar felt remorseful for his involvement in these occurrences, yet he found himself with no alternative as his safety was now at risk. He gestured for the new goalkeeper to approach the team bench, and spoke quietly to his goalkeeper.

"To continue playing football, you must not intervene or take any action. Stay cantered in the goal and avoid committing to either side."

The penalty kick was about to be executed. With a brief run-up, the striker confidently struck the ball. The ball required more precise and powerful striking as it travelled towards the lower centre of the goal. The goalkeeper experienced a sudden moment of confusion when directed to remain in the centre, as the ball approached at a slow, direct trajectory towards the centre. He had only a moment to respond, and allowed the ball to pass cleanly through his legs into the net.

The opposing team secured a 1-0 advantage with 10 minutes remaining in the match, leaving observers unsurprised by the outcome. They refrained from celebrating.

Marko struggled to grasp his role in the game, failing to make a single touch on the ball throughout the match. It is likely that Boris wanted him to participate in the match as an attempt to capitalize on his opponent's lack of stamina and limited training sessions over the past nine months, thus increasing the chances of a victory.

The game promptly resumed from midfield. Both teams achieved their desired outcomes, however, there were still a few minutes remaining in the game. The opponent attempted to control the ball, aiming to maintain possession and secure victory with limited time remaining in the game. Following an ineffective pass from the opposing team, the ball inadvertently ended up at Marko's feet. Despite his instinct to advance, his teammates failed to provide any off-ball movement to offer passing options. Marko was positioned approximately 40 meters away from the opponent's goal at that point in time. He executed a sudden, dynamic sprint towards the ball. He swiftly maneuvered past two opposing players with a quick dribble. Marko observed that the opponent's goalkeeper had strayed far from the goal as the game neared its end. Marko opted to attempt a daring chip shot from a distance of roughly 25 meters. He vigorously powers the ball towards the goal. As the ball swiftly approached the goal, Boris's voice rang out from the stands with a firm, "Nooooooo."

Marko was reminded of his obligation to Boris and his duties on the field. He failed to remember the agreement he had made with Boris. Perhaps unconsciously, he instinctively chose to aim for that exceptional shot, reflecting the core values deeply ingrained in his being. The ball sailed past the goalkeeper into the top left corner of the goal, levelling the score at 1-1 with just a few minutes remaining in the match.

There was no celebration among the members of the Marko team; instead, they all gazed at him in disbelief. There were no further opportunities to score another goal in the remaining minutes. The match ended in a 1-1 draw.

Following the referee's final whistle, Marko experienced a sense of satisfaction, despite breaking his agreement with club owner Boris.

He experienced a surge of joy as he engaged in his favourite activity, finally scoring a goal after a prolonged absence from the football field. Marko entered the dressing room, which was filled with absolute silence. No words were spoken to him; the players hurriedly changed their clothes and swiftly exited the stadium. It was widely understood that the situation did not conclude as expected...

Chapter 22
Fatal Mistake

Upon returning home from the game, Marko experienced extreme fatigue and exhaustion.

After a nine-month hiatus from training, he played a full 90-minute game and experienced soreness in every muscle. A few hours post-game, he struggled to walk due to physical discomfort.

Marko opted to visit the nearby market around 7 pm in order to purchase a meal. On the route to the market near his residence, there was a large and picturesque park located in front of the building.

In the evening, the park was consistently vacant, with only the residents of Marko's building seen walking there.

As Marko was strolling through the park on his way to the market, two large men in black jackets suddenly appeared from the bushes.

They were tall individuals who wore black hoods that concealed their faces up to their eyes. Marko was promptly apprehended and taken to the nearby parking area.

The cloth was placed over Marko's mouth to prevent him from calling for assistance. One of the abductors unlocked the vehicle and forcibly placed Marko inside the trunk.

Marko was visibly terrified and stunned, trembling as he was wedged into the trunk of the car. The vehicle departed the area quickly. Before Marko realized it, he had already travelled a considerable distance from the city in the car's trunk.

The two large, bald individuals halted the vehicle at a specific spot, bound Marko's hands, secured the cloth over his face, and returned him to the trunk.

They continued driving for approximately one hour. Marko was unaware of the identity of his kidnapper and the reason for his abduction.

Upon completing a lengthy journey, the vehicle came to a halt in front of the quaint mountain cottage.

Marko was unsure of his location.

He suffered from blindness and had his hands bound with a rope behind him. He was roughly and aggressively extracted from the trunk.

Marko heard one of the men shout: "Get out your dirty ass, someone wants to meet you."

They took him inside the cottage and uncovered his eyes. Marko was unable to believe what had happened due to the shock.

Boris stood in front of him, casually enjoying a drink, smoking a cigar, and effortlessly throwing darts at the same time.

"You should have heeded my advice, young man. Why did you breach the agreement?"

"I am a professional football player, not someone who deceives," responded Marko.

"Your irresponsible actions have resulted in significant financial and reputational harm to me. My business associates are extremely disheartened by the results of the football match. I betrayed their confidence. Due to your significant error."

"It was not an error; I scored the goal, as footballers are expected to do," Marko confidently stated.

Boris gently placed his whiskey glass on the wooden table next to him and approached Marko slowly. Two bodyguards assisted Marko by holding him under the arm while his hands remained restrained. Boris forcefully grabbed Marko and extinguished his cigar on his face, causing Marko to scream and shout for approximately 20 seconds. "You will be living for the next 72 hours. During that time, your brother is expected to give me 1 million euros in cash. That's all that remains for your hope."

Marko had no clue of the distance from his city and where he was. After the dirty, grey cloth was lifted from his eyes, he found himself inside an abandoned, incomplete house that had been visibly unoccupied for an extended period.

Through a small window, Marko noticed that there were no other houses in close proximity, which suggested that he was in secluded mountainous regions with access to bare dirt roads.

It seemed unlikely that anyone would hear him if he called out for help. As Marko contemplated his next steps, he heard footsteps drawing near and was advised to remain calm and not attempt to escape.

"The nearest residence and road are located miles away, we are in remote location, nobody is coming to save you, boy. Your greatest opportunity for survival lies in exercising wisdom and following the instructions provided. If you attempt to act like a hero, I will eliminate you discreetly, like a dog, ensuring no one ever discovers the truth." Boris intended to intimidate Marko, who remained silent in response.

Marko would advise his brother Nikola against offering money to Boris in return for sparing his life, if only he could. Marko chose not to involve his brother in the difficult situation.

Marko was subjected to physical assault by Boris and his intimidating bodyguards, who punched him repeatedly in the stomach and face. Marko was covered in blood and experiencing significant disorientation, indicating a state of partial unconsciousness. Unable to defend himself, he believed his ribs were fractured and his nose was bleeding profusely.

Chapter 23
The Phone Call

Nikola noticed an incoming call on his phone from an unrecognized number.

"Hello, who is calling?" Nikola inquired when he answered the call.

There was a moment of silence before Nikola repeated, "Can you hear me? Who is calling?"

Meanwhile, Boris held a gun to Marko's head and instructed him to speak on the phone.

After a brief pause, Marko murmured into the phone, "Nik...I apologize for not heeding your advice. Forgive me. Refrain from giving them any money, in exchange for my life. Please do it like that Nik."

"Marko, are you the one speaking? Where are you? Is everything alright?" Nikola fell to his knees in shock.

Marko's speech was ambiguous, indicating to Nikola that he was potentially at risk.

Boris took a phone and finally started talking to Nikola. "Congratulations on your accomplishment; we are pleased and proud of your success, boy. You are now able to assist me by attentively listening. I hold no grievances against your brother, nothing personal. The issue at hand is the significant amount of money blown away because of your brother recently, which now necessitates prompt resolution of the resulting debt. You are required to deliver 1,000,000 euros in cash within 72 hours. Do not ask questions or attempt to outsmart us; simply listen if you wish to see your brother again."

"Please do not harm my brother!"

Boris replied in a sarcastic way: "I cannot bear the thought of causing harm to anyone. As an entrepreneur and businessman, I strive to conduct myself in a manner that does not cause harm to others. I would say, at least in most cases. Therefore, it is imperative that you closely follow my instructions in order to ensure the well-being of your brother." "Refrain from contacting law enforcement as it may result in harm to your brother. Additionally, there are no individuals within law enforcement who are willing to offer you assistance, believe me. It is advisable to approach situations with increased intelligence and practicality in order to achieve a win win outcome. Simply arrange the necessary funds and board the next available flight. Upon your arrival, I will contact you to provide further instructions. Keep in mind that you should have 1,000,000 euros in cash at your disposal, a 72-hour time frame, and the stipulation of avoiding involving law enforcement. Please consider your next move thoughtfully, Nikola," Boris concluded the call.

"Hello! Can you hear me? Marko!" Nikola dropped to his knees in the midst of the bustling streets of Lisbon.

He was sobbing and yelling loudly. What has happened to Marko? Why did his brother get abducted?

After few seconds, he rose from the ground, recognizing the urgency of the situation. Nikola needed to prepare quickly because his brother was in a dangerous situation and required assistance.

Nikola was uncertain about the course of action to take, his disorganized thought process severely hindered his cognitive clarity and decision-making abilities. He was aware that contacting the police was not an option, as many officers had been influenced by Boris's corruption. Nikola just followed his gut instinct and took a cash from the bank. He hurried to the airport and boarded the next flight.

Chapter 24
The Clock Is Ticking

Upon landing from airport, Nikola promptly contacted Boris.

"I just landed. Please indicate the location where you would like me to deliver the funds. I also seek reassurance about my brother's well-being," Nikola asserted confidently.

"The big boy has arrived, I see....Well, don't you worry, all is well, we eagerly anticipated your presence. Rest assured, your brother is safe and you will be reunited with him shortly. Please pay close attention to my instructions without any distractions or hidden games. You will have the opportunity to meet my friend. He will be waiting for you outside the restaurant 'Gold' in one hour time. Just a gentle reminder that contacting the authorities would result in the permanent disappearance of your brother. I think you are understood."

Nikola left airport contemplating whether or not to contact police. A small part of him retained hope that there were still honourable law enforcement officers who would carry out their duties with integrity.

Nikola was aware that contacting the authorities could potentially lead to Boris discovering the situation and harming his brother. Nikola experienced a sense of powerlessness in the challenging and stressful circumstances.

Before boarding a taxi to depart, Nikola paused to sit on a bench and ponder for a moment. When police inspector Zdravko visited his brother in jail, Nikola remembered telling him about that police officer. When Marko was released from jail, he told his brother, Nikola, about an encounter with a police officer who had come to his aid. At that moment, police officer Zdravko was conducting a thorough investigation into the activities of notorious drug mafia leader Boris. Nikola was informed of the matter by his brother Marko. However, despite Nikola's trust in the police inspector, he still required the inspector's phone number and time was running out.

Nikola quickly made up his mind, he planned to contact the sincere and honourable police officer for advice, as he was likely the only one fulfilling his duties properly. Without delay, Nikola went to the apartment hoping to find the phone number of inspector Zdravko.

After a 20-minute taxi journey from the airport, Nikola arrived at the apartment. He swiftly searched through the apartment for the phonebook directory. Nikola was aware of his brother Marko's reputation for being systematic and storing all phone numbers in a notebook. Despite searching every corner of the apartment, Nikola could not locate the notebook with the phone numbers. Upon the brink of surrender, he stumbled upon a list containing more than 100 phone numbers inside the drawer adjacent to Marko's bedside.

Nikola was thrilled to find a written phone contact labelled 'Police inspector Zdravko' along with a corresponding number.

In an instant, Nikola dialled the phone number..."Hello, I apologize for the interruption."

"Boris, the leader of the mafia, has kidnapped and subjected my brother to torture. My name is Nikola, his sibling. According to Marko, you paid a visit to him while in jail and he complimented you for being a good police officer.

"Hi, Nikola. It's fortunate that you were able to locate my contact information and reach out to me. In the previous year, I have collected all the evidence related to Boris. I'm unsure if you're keeping up with the political developments in Serbia, but the ruling political party was defeated last week after 8 years in power. The Democrats have assumed control, leaving Boris devoid of any remaining protections. It is now the great moment to apprehend him.

"Sir, I am concerned, if Boris detects police intervention, he will eliminate Marko. I must meet his bodyguard within the next 5 minutes; please provide instructions on how to proceed."

"Done be afraid, Nikola. Right now, I am at your service. I received assistance from the police department after providing substantial evidence implicating Boris. This serves as a compelling demonstration of the decision to incarcerate him for an extended period. You must meet with him at the designated restaurant," he instructed Nikola. "I will locate your phone to determine your location prior to your meeting with Boris. You may proceed with bringing the money as originally intended. Upon arrival, we will be strategically positioned in close proximity, diligently observing for the opportune moment to apprehend Boris and his associates. I am en route to provide you with a discreet microphone equipped with GPS. I will conceal it under your armpit to gather additional evidence when you reach Boris."

"I am scared, what if they find out?" "Nikola expressed concern about potential issues if the microphone is discovered."

"Rest assured, that is not a concern you need to fret over. It is undetectable by the naked eye and cannot be sensed by any sensor, so you will not be affected. We require access to your discussion with Boris in order to determine the most opportune moment to intervene. There is no need to worry, as the elite squad will carry out the operation, leading to the apprehension of Boris."

Shortly thereafter, Police Inspector Zdavko implanted a small chip beneath Nikola's arm.

Zdravko demonstrated strong qualities as a police officer, earning the trust of Nikola. Following the conclusion of operational plan discussions, Nikola went to the restaurant 'Gold' to meet with Boris's bodyguard. En route, Nikola hailed a taxi to reach the establishment where he found three sizable individuals donning black jackets and suits, leisurely sipping coffee. Upon noticing Nikola, they promptly rose from their seats at the table and proceeded to make their way towards their vehicle parked on the opposite side of the street. Nikola trailed closely behind them, staying within a few meters of distance. Nikola entered the car without speaking to the criminals. After an hour-long journey, they reached their destination. Nikola mentally braced himself for the impending challenges, recognizing the tough road ahead. Exiting the car, he made his way towards the secluded mountain dwelling. It was located a considerable distance from civilization.

As he approached the entrance, he noticed his brother Marko lying on the floor in the centre of the room, gripping onto the large metal beam above him. Marko exhibited visible signs of torture and physical abuse, indicating potential internal injuries. Within the residence, there were a total of five bodyguards present, along with Boris.

Nikola advanced cautiously, under close scrutiny from Boris's security team.

"Well, well, well, look who decided to show up," Boris remarked, clapping his hands slowly and sarcastically.

"It appears we're having a family gathering after all. Finally, Nikola makes a reappearance. I understand that you may feel frustrated as my decision could potentially disrupt your promising football career; however, there are values that hold greater significance than financial gain. Nik, do you share my opinion?"

Boris carried on with his conversation as he loaded his gun.

"I consider myself to be a pleasant individual. You may have differing views, but you have not observed my friendly personality. You may be wondering why all of this is occurring at the moment. If your brother wasn't smart ass, I wouldn't have to do this."

Nikola noticed his brother displaying signs of severe injuries.

"Here is your payment, 1 million euro in cash. The agreement is now completed. Let us depart now, Boris; I must transport my brother to the hospital to prevent him from succumbing to his injuries" Nikola declared as he set the bag of money down and took a few steps forward.

"Certainly, Nikola, certainly. Do people view me as someone who doesn't stick to their agreements? Your brother will recover, he simply required a minor adjustment in his behaviour. You see, I serve as a mentor for you both, teaching valuable lessons through real-life examples on protecting what you admire and supporting your vision."

Nikola, do you have an understanding of it? You see, we are the same. Your arrival today was confirmation aimed at safeguarding your values, regardless of the sacrifice you had to make along the way.

I also prioritize protecting my business at all costs, as evident in my actions, boy . Are we alike in your opinion?

"Boris then circled around Marko, pointing his gun at him in every direction. I am releasing your brother, Nikola. There is just one final task remaining for me to complete. I am committed to fulfilling the promise I made to your brother about ending his football career, as I am a man of my word..." Boris paused as he approached Marko and rested the gun against his left knee.

"This encounter will leave a lasting impression on you, serving as a cherished memory for years to come. Your football career will be permanently ended by my little gift. A modest gift from me in response to your desire to fully understand the challenges of earning respect."

Moments later, Boris shot Marko in the left knee. Marko let out a powerful scream that conveyed the intensity of the pain he was experiencing. Nikola was forced to witness his brother's agonizing screams while being held mercilessly on the ground.

At that moment, law enforcement officers forcefully entered the residence. The elite special police force tactically breached the building from multiple entry points, commanding those inside to freeze and lie down on the floor as instructed by Police Inspector Zdravko over the megaphone.

As the police officers approached Boris, he made the decision to draw his gun and fire at them. Despite his efforts, the Special Police Force Team was swift to knock him down before he could even lift his weapon, ultimately killing him on the spot.

The remaining members of the gang were promptly subdued and apprehended on the ground.

An ambulance stood at the ready near the residence, and Marko was swiftly transported by the medical team on a stretcher.

"Nikola, how are you holding up?" inquired Police Inspector Zdravko.

"Will my brother survive? Have I done enough to save Marko?"

The outcome is now entrusted to dear Lord," Zdravko replied.

"Your assistance is greatly appreciated, sir. I had an intuition that you were a decent individual," Nikola responded to the police inspector, stating that there are still honourable individuals in our nation who proudly wear the uniform.

Prior to Boris's decision to abduct Marko, the government had collapsed a few weeks earlier. The outdated political system began to be dismantled with the inauguration of the new government.

Given the circumstances, police inspector Zdravko was granted full autonomy to carry out the arrest of Boris and other individuals involved in criminal activities.

Zdravko was suspended by the prior administration for attempting to uncover their connections with mafia leaders throughout the nation. With the implementation of the new ruling system, individuals such as Boris no longer had the benefit of protection.

As a result, Boris was finally subject to numerous charges brought against him, prompting his attempt to resist arrest by firing at police officers as he sought to evade imprisonment.

However, justice was ultimately served. Marko underwent three weeks of intensive care in the hospital before eventually recovering, showcasing the universe's ability to restore balance at the end of a painful journey.

Together, he and his brother Nikola relocated to Portugal.

Marko suffered irreversible knee injury, rendering him unable to continue playing football. However, he was content to be alive and had the privilege of actively supporting his brother Nikola in his great football career.

Epilogue

The fictional narrative features multiple fictional characters, yet is inspired by real events.

Marko reflects the reality that many talented young players fall short of their potential due to a lack of focus and self-discipline. A significant proportion of gifted soccer players did not live up to their potential and failed to achieve their goals due to a lack of determination and dedication.

Marko's character demonstrates that talent alone is insufficient without the capacity to uphold strong work ethics and confront our inner struggles daily, it serves as a prime example of our need for constant self-improvement and pursuit of personal growth on a daily basis.

On opposite hand, Marko's brother, Nikola, exemplifies how persistent effort and a determined mindset can have a more profound positive impact than talent alone.

Nikola exemplifies the importance of uncovering our individual talents and potential that may be latent within us.

Once we identify our strengths and become familiar with our individual talents, we must adopt a warrior mentality and be prepared to endure occasional setbacks.

We need to anticipate that there will be individuals testing our commitment to maintaining the achievements of our aspirations. The more challenging the journey towards our aspirations, the more remarkable the ultimate success will be.

Many mafia bosses and gang members have close connections with politicians and the government, as Boris does.

Yet, we have a perfect mechanism in our universe to maintain long-term balance, which is fortunate.

All people have the freedom to engage in any activity of their choosing, but are unable to control the duration of such activities.

The ultimate consequence for individuals who have done wrong is the undeniable fact that no matter how fierce the storm may be, the ocean will eventually calm.

Individuals such as mafia leader Boris serve as a test of our resilience and determination, challenging us to assess the sacrifices we are willing to make in pursuit of our objectives.

In order to achieve long-term success and reach our goals, we must overcome any obstacles that come our way.

Despite facing challenging circumstances, we must persist until the very end, football remains the world's most popular sport, with top teams valued at billions of dollars and commanding a loyal following worldwide.

Furthermore, football plays a crucial role in shaping a shared identity, uniting individuals across diverse communities in their passion for the sport.

Yet, in recent years, several diligent studies have exposed a concerning lack of integrity within the industry, football has been marked by infiltration and corruption, giving rise to malpractice, deviance, and criminal behaviour. The industry's sizable financial allure makes it a prime target for criminal organizations seeking to profit and launder illegal funds.

These groups seek to amass power, influence, and control through acts of intimidation, protection, and ultimately through violence or corruption.

Criminal organizations use football as a means to enhance their reputation and influence through various legal and illegal activities.

Some groups may even infiltrate youth soccer teams by funding young players, or providing financial assistance.

Mafia groups utilize personal connections to manipulate match outcomes and profit from illicit betting networks.

In today's sport, a network of players, referees, and managers has been implicated in a corrupt system that benefits specific clubs.

Allegations of money laundering and fraud persist at the highest levels, yet, it remain public secret, with hidden evidence.

To combat corruption in football and restore public trust, enhanced governance structures are imperative at both local and national levels.

It is positive news that FIFA, the international governing body, plans to reinstate the corruption offense in its ethics code, which had previously been removed.

Improved oversight and transparency are also necessary for the significant financial resources attracted by the industry. It is imperative for FIFA and national governing bodies to supervise team and player transfers, regulate legal betting, and enforce transparency in sponsorship programs.

Additionally, it is important to note that the sports sector may unintentionally mean of finance for organized crime syndicates and criminal organizations, while also providing economic opportunities for unethical businesspeople.

In order to address this issue, organizations like UEFA must establish expertise and implement measures to combat corruption, while also retaining the ability to monitor and impose disciplinary actions within the industry.

A soccer field serves as a gathering spot for various interests and individuals, it is a multifunctional environment for business, entertainment, and competition.

True leadership in these industries necessitates integrity, commitment, and a commitment to benefit the majority, rather than enriching a select few.

Tomorrow is Always a New Day

Strive to exceed your current capabilities and emerge as the ultimate winner. No matter what happens, stay determined to keep pushing forward, regardless of the obstacles that may arise. To be victorious, you must embrace all your abilities ability to overcome any challenge.

In challenging times and in the face of others' attempts to restrict you, remain calm in your mindset, rather than being deterred by doubts of your abilities.

Use these challenges to fuel your determination and commitment, understanding that success lies in the journey rather than the final destination. Even after accomplishing your goals, you need to continue to strive for higher levels of potential and reach new heights of success.

You are a wonderfully created, and it is your duty to discover and enhance your own unique talents.

It is never too late to embark on the path to success. Always keep in mind that choosing to progress despite challenges and making a consistent effort towards personal development is of greater significance than any accomplishments you may achieve. Keep that winning mindset.

Strive to exceed your boundaries and shatter barriers holding you back.

There is no such moment in life when we can't go forward anymore; we must remain resilient until our final accomplishments.

In life, no end goal will equal a finishing line. There is no race to be completed.

We cannot say, "I made it, the race is finished, I am at the mountain's peak. That's a dangerous mindset where we get satisfied with our achievements and lose hunger for further accomplishments."

If we look for that finishing line to 'touch it', we will get into the trap of an endless search that leads nowhere.

Real happiness is in appreciating what we already have and not focusing on things we miss. For every beautiful moment spent with our family and friends, we must capture, appreciate, and steal it from the fast-paced living and make it last as long as possible.

When we are young and shallow, we think that money and fame will give us long-lasting happiness, but life will always find a way to convince us otherwise.

Sometimes, people will put limits on us. I remember we had a school marathon when I was 11 years old. In the morning, at our meeting point, my teacher came up and asked me in front of all the other kids: "Mladen, do you have proper running shoes for this race?" I only had one pair of old clumsy shoes, the ones I used for school, birthday parties, and playing outside on the street. Ashamed and embarrassed, holding my tears back, I answered, "No, I have only this pair of shoes…"

My teacher said, "Look, some other kids are into track and field sports at this time, and they are expected to win this race. Do not get discouraged, because you will not win today."

Indeed, I watched those kids around me; they had brand-new shoes and sports clothes…

About 100 meters before the finish line, I realize that I am still full of energy. I started running as fast as I could…

Shortly, I took the lead and won that race! All my teachers quickly approached me, and instead of greeting me, they were in disbelief and asked me how I managed to win.

Don't ever let someone tell you where your limits are. Don't let anyone wrongly convince you that you are not good enough to achieve your dreams. They don't know what you went through to become who you are today! BELIEVE IN YOURSELF!

Our main character, Nikola, experiences the same problems when people try to put limits on his potential. The shallow and rotten world of the football association did not impact his desire to push the limits and unlock his full potential.

You are beautifully created, and people will always try to put limits on you regardless of what.

Yet, with the right character and warrior mindset, you are ready to break every shark aquarium and prove to everyone your real value.

Our main character, Nikola, did not strive for anything less than brilliance; he did not want to make excuses about his life and circumstances. Instead, he took his destiny into his own hands and moulded his future into brilliance, despite all the difficult things around him.

If you want to do something great, you can always find a way, but if you don't want to, you will always find an excuse.

It is your choice, make the good one! Be the champion and become who you are created to be!